NOT FOR THE FAINT OF HEART

ALSO BY JESSE MAAS

The Desiccant Keepers
Ivy Letters

Not FOR THE Faint of HEART

A Novel By Jesse Maas

Purple Fish Publishing

In Memory of Mamaw & Debbie

I wish you were both still here to read this.

CHAPTERS

Seven Years Ago 1

(Now) A Change of Pace 6

You Have a Latte Nerve 21

Call Me If You Can 26

A Trip Down MarshWalk Lane 47

An Unexpected Swim 65

Gone to Texas 81

First Date Feelings 102

A Fight For The Ages 132

A Serendipitous Occasion 156

Well... This is Awkward 171

Summer Shenanigans 188

I Can't Tonight 206

The Wedding Bells Are Ringing 224

This Simply Cannot Be 258

Everything and Nothing 272

Highs and Lows 281

So It Goes 289

PROLOGUE

Of all the things I've done in my life, this one might be the craziest. The last six months have been unbearable and breathtaking, miserable and mesmerizing. The highs and lows, the ebbs and flows… they've been too much to handle, and this morning was my breaking point.

Or maybe, it was the opposite? What's the opposite of a breaking point? A mountain top moment? I don't know. I'll have to look that up later.

Right now, I just need to run.

ONE

I've only been to my mother's grave once, and it was the day of her burial.

At Dad's request, the morning of the funeral, we all ate breakfast together. Our kitchen was filled to the brim with flowers and baked goods; I don't think our refrigerator could have fit another lasagna. I picked at a blueberry muffin I wasn't interested in eating, while trying to mentally prepare for the day ahead.

The service was held at our church, and it was packed. Mom was very involved in our small town. She was everything you'd picture a Texas-raised woman to be. She baked casseroles for all the church potlucks, volunteered to chaperone the school dances, and of course, baked the town's best chocolate chip cookies. More than *what* she did, it was *who* she was. She was compassionate. She was graceful. And she was faithful. Everyone loved her.

I remember very little of the service. I sat in the front row with Bennett, my older brother, on my right and Grace, my best friend, on my left.

When the service was over, I stood at the back of the church with Dad and Bennett in the receiving line. Dad didn't want a formal wake. He could barely handle seeing everyone at one event, let alone two, so he opted to try to combine them. In a blur, we talked to everyone leaving the church. I remember almost nothing people said… it all sounded the same: "I'm sorry for your loss. Your mother was an amazing woman. She's in a better place." It was all the generic stuff people say when they really have nothing to say. I don't blame them. Death sucks. What can anyone possibly say to make it better? Nothing really.

But boy they can say things to make it worse…

One of my mom's friends ("friend" is probably too strong of a word) had the audacity to tell me, "You're young. You will get over it." I still don't know if it was meant to be encouraging… or what exactly she was trying to get across… but what I *do* know is that some people should *not* be allowed to open their mouths. And she's one of them.

Dad only invited our closest family and friends to go to the gravesite after the service. We sang a couple of songs, prayed, and Dad said a few words, though to this day, I'm still not sure how he possibly held himself together long enough to say anything.

Then, they lowered her casket into the ground. And she was officially gone.

I hated it.

It was one of the worst moments of my life… though it was quickly followed by *the* worst moment of my life.

Slowly but surely, people headed home until it was only Dad, Bennett, Grace, Grandpa (mom's dad), Aunt Marie (dad's sister), and me remaining. I moseyed away from the crowd toward the edge of the cemetery. Large trees lined the border as the ground sloped downward. I watched the leaves blow in the wind and enjoyed the moment alone with my thoughts.

Since she'd died, the days had been filled with people coming and going, talking and consoling, crying and laughing and I'd had very little time to myself.

"I can't believe she's gone," Bennett's soft voice startled me. I turned around to find him standing oddly close with his hands in the pockets of his black slacks. His dirty blonde hair looked unnaturally blonder, like he'd dyed or bleached it, and his light blue eyes had a red glow, a stark contrast to his black attire.

"Me either," I replied in a barely audible whisper.

"It's too bad, you know," his tone suddenly felt edgy.

"What's too bad? That she died?" I candidly asked, annoyed at him.

"That it's *your* fault."

The words felt like a dagger in my chest. I couldn't breathe. I blinked rapidly, trying to find words to say and air to speak them.

"What?" I finally got out.

"You were supposed to be with her… Dad told me. If you hadn't been acting like the brat you've always been, she wouldn't have been there. She wouldn't have died."

The ground beneath my feet no longer felt steady and the air began to swirl around me. I blinked rapidly as tears flowed down my cheeks.

"How could you possibly say that?"

"I can say it because it's true. If it weren't for you, Mom would still be here."

"Coming from you?" I raised my voice. "You're the one with the audacity to show up high to our own mother's funeral!"

He shook his head and his mouth curled up in a callous grin. "Don't put this on me. *You're* the reason she's dead. *You're* the reason we'll never see her again."

I covered my mouth, suddenly nauseous. My chin quivered and my stomach churned. I pulled off my black pumps as quickly as I could and took off running down the cemetery road, desperately trying to push out my brother's cruel words. Desperately trying to convince myself I didn't believe him.

But I did. I still do. He's right.

TWO

I feel the damp sand scrunch beneath my toes as I walk down the nearly empty beach. The tide is coming in but I'm careful not to let the cold water touch my bare feet. Most days, this time of year, I keep my tennis shoes on when I walk, but the weather was warm over the weekend, so I let my feet feel the sand. It's a freeing feeling. There's something about the way an empty beach makes you feel like everything is okay, no matter how *not* okay everything really is.

It's February and I'm thankful the beach is empty. Myrtle Beach is a tourist town at its core. With seafood buffets, mini-golf courses, and a pancake house on every block, if you're looking for a cliché vacation, Myrtle Beach is your spot.

I first moved here two years ago, but before that, I'd never been.

I was graduating from the University of Texas and, after spending the first twenty-two years of my life in the Lone Star state, I wanted to get out. I landed a fully remote job doing graphic design work for a company based in New York City and realized I could live anywhere. Like many millennials would, I Googled "most affordable beach towns" and found Myrtle Beach.

The night started with a full bottle of Moscato and my roommate, Grace, swiping through Tinder. It ended with a $2,000 non-refundable apartment deposit, Grace matching with thirty-five guys "looking for something deeper," and two empty bottles of Moscato. Needless to say, when I woke up the next day to a confirmation email for my twelve-month apartment lease, I was thankful to see that the place at least looked nice. And bonus, I'd reserved the apartment beginning the correct month. A few weeks later, my dad came down to Austin, helped me pack up a small U-Haul, and drove me across the Bible Belt to good ole' South Carolina.

I was anxious on the drive. The closer we got, the more worried I became. On multiple occasions, I asked my dad to turn the car around. When we were only ten minutes out, we passed a wax museum with a gorilla on top of a cityscape, and I told him I *really* wanted to go back home.

"It's okay," he assured me. "Let's check out the

apartment before we make any decisions. If it's bad, we'll figure it out. I'm not going to leave my little girl anywhere unworthy of her."

He's always been that kind of dad; supporting me in everything and always there to catch me if I fall.

We turned off the main drag and down the road, a nice-looking apartment complex came into view (thank goodness). The place was everything modern America deems important when looking for a place to live: pickleball courts (for no one to use), a dog park (for the pet owners who treat their fur-babies like children), and a community pool (for far too old residents to show far too much skin). But, most importantly, and best of all, it was only a half-mile walk to the beach.

Since I moved, I've made it a habit to walk on the beach every morning I can; the only things that stop me are the rain (though not all the time) and early work meetings. Otherwise, I see the sunrise over the Atlantic every single day.

Today, it's cloudy and the sun is still low. It was the kind of sunrise where the colors of the sun light up the sky long before the sun itself is visible. The gray-blue sky was littered with orange and pink streaks among the clouds before the sun peeked out. A layer of clouds stood between the water's edge and the sky and only when the sun was over the first layer of clouds could it be spotted. Mornings like these are my favorites. They're the kind that keep the casual onlookers away… but little do the tourists know that the cloudy mornings are often the most beautiful.

My walk is three miles long. I've always been a habitual person and my morning ritual is no different. I leave my apartment complex and take a left. I walk past the entrance to a brightly colored neighborhood, followed by a few other houses (types many people would refer to as "sketchy") and reach Business Seventeen (also known as Kings Highway). It's important to note that there are two roads known as "Seventeen" in Myrtle Beach and whoever named them is likely to be described as "unimaginative."

There's Business Seventeen, which runs closer to the water, and Bypass Seventeen, which runs parallel further inland. The bypass was designed to help reduce traffic and make it faster for people to get from "point A" to "point B." However, in my humble opinion, it created two separate roads that are now equally annoying and traffic filled.

I cross Seventeen and continue to the nicer side of the road. Being east of Seventeen can increase your home's value by hundreds of thousands of dollars (unless, of course, you're south of Forty-Eighth Avenue, where the crime rates skyrocket, but that's beside the point). Myrtle Beach is a complex place.

I walk down the residential street and through the public parking lot to the water's edge. I take a right and walk along the sand, past beachfront hotels, until I reach the beginning of the Golden Mile. The Golden Mile is a mostly residential portion of the beach and is relatively quiet and empty. For a portion of my walk, there are beachfront cabanas that are no more than two-hundred square feet a piece. They're brightly colored, as one would expect to find by the ocean, and contain a wet bar, bathroom and sitting area. You're not allowed to spend the night in one (though who would ever know) and I don't really understand the purpose, though evidently my dad does. When he came to visit me the first time after I'd settled in, he saw one was for sale and made an offer. Thankfully, he was outbid. I didn't have the heart to tell him how ridiculous I thought the purchase would have been.

I make it to the last cabana, my turnaround point, and feel my phone start to vibrate. I pull it out from the edge of my waistband and see that Grace is calling. It's only 6:45 a.m. her time, which worries me. She never calls this early. I swipe the screen and lift the phone to my ear. Before I can say a word, she's already halfway through her rant.

"Left without saying a word. Can you believe him?" she cries.

I want to say, "No, I can't believe that." But I can. Grace is beautiful. She's the kind of beautiful that radiates from the inside out. She has luscious, dark brown hair that falls perfectly to her collarbone and is somehow unaffected by all humidity. Her light brown skin is accented by her syrup-colored eyes and almost unnaturally perfect smile. She comes from a family of new money but has the audacity to still be one of the most generous people I've ever met. Thankfully, I met her when I was three, before anyone who really deserved her could take my place as best friend. Her one flaw: she trusts everyone.

"I'm sorry, Grace." There's no use telling her she deserves better than the usual bums she settles for.

"I'm coming to Myrtle Beach," she declares.

"When?"

I'm thankful we don't have to dwell on the boy who left her this time. I can't even remember his name. Eric? Sam? I honestly don't know.

"I'm boarding the plane right now."

It doesn't matter if I have plans or not. After twenty-one years of friendship, I know my place and I am not the decision maker.

"How long are you staying?"

"Oh, sorry, I think they're saying we need to turn our phones off now. See you soon."

She ignores my question and worse than that, she lies. I know she's on her parent's private plane. She hasn't flown commercially since they bought it when we were in middle school. It means she's coming to visit indefinitely.

It happened like this one time before.

Our freshman year of college, I went to the University of Texas and Grace went to Baylor. Halfway through our first semester, she called and told me she was visiting for the weekend, and she never left. We ended up graduating as Longhorns together three and a half years later.

As I walk back to my apartment, I send an email to my boss to let her know something came up and I'll be taking a personal day. If Grace is really here to stay, we'll have a long day ahead of us.

I get cleaned up and decide on jeans and a white, button-down long sleeve. I apply a light layer of mascara and powder foundation and call it good. My Keurig was heating up while I showered and is now ready for my first of the probably four cups of coffee I'll drink today. My usual breakfast consists of two scrambled eggs with cheese and whatever sweet carb item I'm into at the time. This week it's chocolate chip mini muffins.

I eat breakfast and sip my coffee on the balcony of the apartment. It's not very big but it comfortably fits the two wooden chairs and small table I bought from Ikea. While I eat, I calculate what time I'll need to leave to pick Grace up. Fortunately, she's visited before, and I know not to pick her up at Myrtle Beach International Airport. Although, according to me, "international" is a bit of a stretch, considering it only flies direct to Canada. It's kind of like when an event claims a "celebrity" appearance and it's a guy you half recognize from a season of Survivor that aired fifteen years ago. True but also, a bit exaggerated.

Grand Strand Airport is where the private jets come in and Google says it's eighteen minutes away. She called me forty-five minutes ago. It's about a two-hour flight. So, I need to leave in about an hour. Perfect. Plenty of time to still enjoy my morning.

* * *

"Emma!" Grace squeals with delight as she throws her arms around me.

"Grace!" I hug her back with the same enthusiasm.

A man I haven't seen before carries Grace's bags to the back of my car. He must be someone they hired for the day. It's a funny site, per usual, the two of us together. Her Louis Vuitton luggage doesn't quite match the 2009 Ford Focus I drive, but you know what they say, "a brunette and a blonde with an inseparable bond," and that part is emphatically true.

"Sorry for barging in on you like this," she says but doesn't mean it.

"You know you're welcome anytime," I say and do mean it.

"Thank you," Grace waves at the man as he softly shuts the trunk and heads back toward the building. She opens the passenger door and I follow her lead, making my way back to the driver's side.

As I get in the car, she takes me in for the first time.

"Oh, Emma," she sighs. "You're lucky I'm here. You're one shampoo away from becoming a complete frizzy mess." She grabs a piece of my wavy hair and tosses it. "Did you not switch to the moisturizing shampoo I recommended?"

I can't think of an excuse fast enough and before I'm able to respond, Grace is tapping away on her phone. "It will be here tomorrow. Thank God for Amazon Prime."

I learned a long time ago it's best to let Grace go. There's no use in me politely telling her she doesn't need to buy stuff for me. She's going to buy it and I'm going to use it. That's how we work.

I wait for her to speak; to tell me the real reason she's here.

"He left me, Em. I woke up this morning to a text. A freaking text message. Is that what this world has come to?"

Being twenty-something sucks these days. You used to be able to meet people out in public… like at a bar or a sporting event or even the grocery store. But now, if you graduate college and filter through your work colleagues without meeting your special someone… it's only a matter of time before you find yourself downloading a dating app and hoping for the best.

"I'm sorry, Em. A text message after three months…" I roll my eyes. "Eric didn't deserve you." While I was waiting at the airport, I scrolled through her social media feed to refresh my memory.

"Yeah!" she agrees. "He's the worst. I just need a fresh start."

"How *fresh* are we talking?"

She hesitates. "Myrtle Beach fresh?" she somehow poses it as both a question and a statement.

I glance at her. I only have one second to make my look count while I try to keep my eyes on the road.

"Please," she begs. "You have a two-bedroom apartment, and you don't even need it."

"I use the second bedroom as my office. I work in there every day." I don't even know why I'm defending it. I know I'll let her stay.

"But there's that built-in desk in the living room. You can use that."

I sigh. "What are you going to do?" I ask though I

already know the answer. She works part-time as an assistant for her dad's wildly successful company, though I use the term "assistant" lightly. She does basically nothing at all, and I'm fairly certain her dad only employed her to make himself feel better about completely financially supporting his grown daughter.

"I can work remotely. I'll put a desk in my bedroom."

My bedroom? She's already mentally moved in.

"Are you sure you want to move to Myrtle Beach? It's not exactly the kind of town you're used to."

"It wasn't the kind of place *you* were used to either. But look at you now – you're thriving!"

She knows it's not true, but she thinks the compliment will be the final touch to get me to agree. She's right.

She can't stand moments of silence that stretch too long. She continues, "I need a fresh start, and you're it. Pleeease, Emma. You're my best friend, and I need you right now. And I know you need me. Pretty please?" she blinks her eyes like a begging puppy dog.

"Where are we shopping first?" I ask, and she knows this means I'm agreeing she can stay.

* * *

After a day filled with shopping and re-organizing the apartment, I put a frozen pizza in the oven and Grace opens a bottle of rosé.

The place is a mess. I'm halfway through cleaning out the second bedroom and rearranging my new desk. The living room and kitchen are an open concept, and the desk is built along the wall to the right.

Before today, I hadn't used the desk for anything (except to occasionally set mail and packages on). The second bedroom was my office. I could close the door and have some space. It made me feel like I could separate my work life from my personal life.

But… not anymore.

I keep reminding myself it's okay. Grace is more important.

I shift items back and forth on the desk as my mind tries to figure out how to cram the entire contents of a twelve by fourteen-foot room onto a six-foot desk.

Grace's luggage is strewn across the spare bedroom, along with loads of shopping bags. She's planning to sleep on an air mattress for the next week until her new furniture is delivered.

She pours me a generous glass of wine and herself a slightly larger one.

"Cheers," she holds up her glass, "to besties reunited once again."

"Cheers," I raise my glass and clink it to hers.

"Okay, well… now that we're settled–"

"Settled?" I interrupt her and dramatically look around the pit that is currently my – no, *our* – apartment.

"How are you? What's new?" she asks but we talk all the time, so she already knows nothing is new.

"Nothing really."

"How about on the relationship front? You've had to meet some nice guys around here. You live on the beach. What about a lifeguard?"

"No. I don't know…" I stumble over my words. "It's so hard to meet people."

I get up to get a glass of water, in hopes she'll move on from the subject, but she doesn't.

"Get on Tinder," she suggests.

I shake my head 'no' as I fill up my glass.

"You seem so…" she trails off, but I know the word she wants to say is "lonely."

The truth is I haven't made a new friend in… well, let's just say a lot of years. And if it weren't for Grace in college, I probably wouldn't have met anyone at all. I used to make friends all the time… but somewhere along the way it got harder to meet people. "Somewhere…" as if I don't know exactly when it got harder.

"Why don't you get a job at like… a coffee shop or something? Somewhere you can meet people?"

"I have a job."

"But you don't meet people."

"I'm not going to go work at a coffee shop. I make enough money and my job keeps me busy enough."

That's the thing about working for a New York City-based company. It pays a nice Manhattan salary, but the work culture comes along with it. It's not quite the same as the hometown Texas environment I was used to when I graduated.

"A bar," she suggests.

"Too sketchy."

"A hotel?"

"The people wouldn't be staying in Myrtle."

"Babysitting?"

"Do you want me to date a four-year-old?"

"Car dealership?"

I bust out laughing.

"Oh my gosh!" I open my mouth excitedly. "That's it! I'm going to work at a car dealership!"

Now, we're both laughing.

"I'm just saying… I want you to get back out there. Meet a nice guy. Meet anyone."

"I have you."

She gets up off the couch and walks to the kitchen. She wraps her arms around me, and I take a sip of water, not remotely reciprocating the hug.

"And you always will. Just think about it. Please, for me?"

I wiggle out of her hold. I've never been one for physical affection.

"I'll think about it."

And for the first time, I wonder if she really came to Myrtle Beach for her… or if she came for me.

THREE

A few weeks pass and we settle into a new normal. Grace's furniture arrives and her bedroom now looks like a misplaced Pottery Barn ad inside our otherwise average apartment.

I must admit, it's been nice having her around. Sometimes, you don't realize how lonely you are until you're not lonely anymore. Then, you're left wondering how you spent so many nights binge watching your favorite television shows while rolling your eyes at Netflix continually asking you if you're "still watching?"

Thankfully, Grace has never been a morning person, so I've been able to continue my walking routine. This morning, the beach is narrow, and I pay more attention to where I'm stepping. The sand is soft, and it always surprises me how easily I could roll an ankle. But maybe that's just me… I'm not the most coordinated person in the world.

It's Saturday so the beach is busier this morning and I dread what it means: tourist season is upon us. It's early March and spring breaks must be starting. From now until Easter, we will have a fairly steady stream of visitors. It will slow down a bit until Memorial Day and then the floodgates will open, and our quiet beach town will become the focal point of millions of people's summer vacations.

From Memorial Day to Labor Day, I figure it's best to not go out. Like *ever*. My first summer here, I made the mistake of trying to go out to dinner with my dad when he was in town. One of my favorite spots on the water quoted us a wait time of three hours. *Three hours.* Is that even a real estimate a hostess can give?

I'm walking back through the parking lot of the apartment complex when I see Grace sitting out on our balcony. She stands up when she sees me.

"I need coffee," she groans. "Are you ready to go?" she puts two fingers to her temple and rubs.

"Rough night?" I almost have to shout. Our apartment is on the second floor and I'm still twenty yards from it.

"I don't want to talk about it," I can barely make out

her words. She heads back into the apartment. She's downstairs before I get to the breezeway. "Will you drive?" she hands me the keys to her Range Rover. Her dad had it shipped out here when she decided to make the move official.

"Sure," I grab the keys and we walk to her car. We've always enjoyed checking out local coffee shops and our current favorite is Beach Hippie Coffee. It's an adorable, brightly colored shop with cute, beachy themed drinks.

I order for us both: an almond milk beach bun latte for me and a longboard latte for Grace. Grace grabs a table in the corner for us. She is wearing her sunglasses inside and her hair is disheveled. She might as well be wearing a sign that blatantly says, "I'm hungover." I know better than to ask her what happened last night before she's gotten her morning coffee in her, so I watch the people and take in the shop. There's a family with five children ordering at the counter and I start to mentally calculate how much their bill will be. I want kids someday… but not *that* many. There are two old men at a table, one reading a book and the other a newspaper, and a dad with his daughter, sharing a cinnamon roll.

Up to my right, I notice a bulletin board with flyers pasted on it. "Annie" is being performed at the local high school in a few weeks and "Shen Yun" will be in Charleston soon.

"Emma," the barista calls my name and one more poster catches my eye. I blink and shake my head. Surely, I'm seeing things. I walk up to get our drinks.

On the way back, I stop and stand eye level with the poster. It has black and white clipart of a girl with a dog and reads: Need a reliable dog walker for your furry best friend? I'm your girl! Along the bottom of the flyer are strips of perforated paper to be easily torn off with a phone number.

My phone number.

I set our cups on the coffee table and rip the flyer off the wall.

"What's this?" I demand, holding the flyer in Grace's face.

She rubs her eyes. Did she actually fall asleep under her sunglasses?

"What's what?" she asks. She moves toward her coffee, but I pull it back so it's out of her reach.

"Not until you explain this." I hand her the flyer.

She moves her sunglasses to the top of her head and examines the flyer as if she's never seen it before.

"I'm not sure what you want me to explain. Are you in need of a dog walker?" she tries to lie but I can see the edges of her lips creasing up. She's suppressing a smile.

"That's *my* phone number and you know it! I told you I didn't want a job. I don't need to meet people." I sit down aggressively in my seat like a little child throwing a tantrum.

"Oh, come on! You love walking… and you love dogs. What's the harm in putting your name out there?"

"I don't *need* my name out there. I don't *need* a job. You're always so controlling."

"Okay, okay. I'm sorry." She knows she's pushed me too far. She looks at the flyer again. "It looks like only two people tore off your number anyway. I'm sure they'll never call."

"Did you hang up any other posters?"

"No, just the one. I didn't want you to get *too* much business," she winks.

I sigh. What did she think would happen if I randomly got a call to walk someone's dog?

FOUR

We spend the rest of the day on the beach with too much sun and too little sunscreen. It was the first truly hot day we'd had of the year, and we wanted to soak it all in.

My skin typically isn't too sensitive to the sun. I normally get one bad sunburn to start the year and then, the rest of the summer, it turns to tan. Unfortunately for me, *this* is the one bad burn.

I sit down on the couch as softly as I can. My burned skin, hot to the touch, stings against the pleather. I know it will hurt again when I stand, but I try not to think about it.

Grace comes out of the bathroom with a pink towel tied around her hair. She's wearing white, silk pajama shorts with a matching top, which accents her light brown skin.

"What's your dinner plan?" she asks.

"I ate while you were showering. I still had some leftover tacos."

"Cool. I couldn't decide, but you helped. I'm going to order Chinese."

She grabs her phone off the kitchen table and walks to her bedroom, half shutting the door behind her. I pick up the remote and turn on the television. My phone is lying face down on couch and I feel it vibrate. I pick it up and see a text from a number I don't have with the local area code.

I unlock my phone and open it.

(843-555-1521) *Hi, I found your number on a flyer. I have a dog and I need someone to walk her. Are you available tomorrow morning?*

I roll my eyes and set my phone down. I hear Grace hang up.

"Suuure… no one will ever call," I obnoxiously say.

"What?"

"The flyer. Someone just texted me about walking their dog tomorrow morning."

"Well," she pauses, "Technically, I'm still right. They didn't call," she laughs.

I roll my eyes again.

"What do I say?"

"Just tell them you can't walk the dog. No harm done."

Ugh. "Okay."

(Me) *Sorry, I am not available tomorrow morning.*

"Want to watch a movie?" Grace asks.

"Sure." I pick up the remote again and start to scroll. "What are you thinking?"

"Maybe, romance?"

My phone vibrates.

(843-555-1521) *Are you available tomorrow afternoon? I really need help. I know it's last minute.*

"Grace, I'm going to kill you!" I shout dramatically.

"What?"

"This person wants to know if I'm available tomorrow afternoon. They said they really need help."

"So, tell them you have plans," Grace shrugs.

"Grace," I whine. I feel sick to my stomach. I don't like to lie. And "no" is hardly used in my vocabulary. "I don't know what to do…"

"Weren't you thinking about trying out that new church tomorrow?"

"I'd thought about it."

"Then, see, you *do* have plans!"

I breathe in heavily. Okay. I *do* have plans. It's not a lie.

(Me) *I'm very sorry but tomorrow is not a great day for me.*

I add the word "very" because I really hate disappointing people.

Grace sits down on the couch.

"Sorry," she laughs through the apology and shrugs.

I don't have anything to say. I know there hasn't *really* been any harm done. I don't even know the person texting me and surely, they'll figure it out.

"So, which should it be: *The Notebook* or *Mean Girls?*"

We pick one of those movies (or really any Rachel McAdams' movie) ninety percent of the time.

My phone starts ringing. Before I even confirm who's calling, I shoot Grace a disapproving look. I'm already positive I know who it will be. I pick up my phone and sure enough, it's the 843 number. I extend my arm to show Grace the screen.

"Look what you did!"

She bites her lip. "Sorry." She smirks like a toddler waiting until his mom gets to two and a half seconds on the count of three before cooperating. "Don't answer it."

I anxiously fidget with my hands and let the phone keep ringing. There's a pit in my stomach. I don't like ignoring people.

Finally, the ringing stops.

"Thanks a lot," I mutter as Grace continues to search for a movie.

My phone starts ringing again.

"Oh my gosh!"

Grace can't control herself anymore. She busts out laughing. "I never expected this to happen."

The reality sinks in. I have to answer it. Evidently, they're desperate. And for some reason, I appear to be the only answer to their desperation. Is this one of those "a lack of planning on your part doesn't constitute an emergency on mine" kind of thing? I really hope so.

I take a deep breath and get up off the couch.

"Are you going to answer it?" Grace asks, her tone filled with surprise.

I ignore her question and walk to my bedroom. I'm too flustered to acknowledge my stinging, sunburned legs as they peel off the couch. I'm not going to talk to the person with Grace right next to me. I don't want to give her the satisfaction. I swipe the screen to answer and shut the door to my room.

"Hello."

"Hi," a woman's voice greets on the other end of the line. Her voice sounds scratchy and well-used; like a good record played over and over again. "Sorry, to call. I'm just not great at texting. My name's Louise."

"Hi, Louise. I'm Emma."

"Listen, I'm sorry to keep bothering you but I'm really in a tight spot. I'm looking for someone to walk my dog every morning for the next six weeks or so."

Six weeks? Are you kidding me?

"Oh… I um…" I try to speak but she doesn't seem to notice. I pace the room as she continues to talk.

"My husband just had a terrible back surgery, and he has to stay in the hospital for a while, followed by a number of weeks in rehab. He's normally the one to walk our dog. I'm old. I'll be seventy-four next year and I have a bad hip, so I can't do it."

How am I supposed to say "no" to this woman? I'll tell her I have another job and can't commit to that much. That will be fine.

But… I've always had a soft spot for the elderly.

"She's a five-year old Corgi named Daisy. We got her when she was a puppy… and that was probably a bad idea, considering our age… but we love her, and we need someone to help us take care of her. Do you think you'd be able to help me out tomorrow?"

"Sure, I can be there tomorrow." The words come out before I can even think them.

"Wonderful! We can talk about future plans in the morning, and how much you'd like to be paid. If you could be here at nine, that would be great. I'm not much of a morning person, but I should be able to make that work. I will text you the address."

Future plans? I only committed to tomorrow.

"Okay, that sounds great!" I reply but really, it sounds strictly average.

"Thanks so much! I appreciate it. I'll see you in the morning."

"See you tomorrow. Bye bye."

"Goodbye."

I hang up the phone and stand still, my jaw slightly dropped. What just happened?

I mope out of the bedroom and to the couch, letting out a long, exaggerated sigh the entire way. I flop myself facedown onto the chaise and pull a pillow to my face.

"Why do I say 'yes' to everything?" I ask Grace as I hit my head to the pillow repeatedly.

She starts laughing. "So, saying 'no' didn't go as planned?"

I glare up at her. "Why are you laughing? This is *your* fault. It was some poor old woman on the phone, and she sounded completely desperate."

"At least you'll get out and meet someone." She winks.

"I thought you wanted me to meet a nice guy. I can't date a seventy-three-year-old woman," I laugh.

Although I *want* to be mad at Grace, and the whole situation, surprisingly, I'm not too upset. I only agreed to *one* walk… and I *do* love corgis…. surely, it won't be that bad.

Maybe, it will even be fun.

* * *

I map Louise's house on my phone, and it says it's a seven-minute drive. At 8:45 a.m., I start making my second cup of coffee in a travel mug. The Keurig starts sputtering, dispensing the last drops, and I grab my cup when it's finished. I take the car keys off the hook and head out the door.

The hallway to our apartment is open-air and I feel the humidity like a wave. I'm not excited about making the transition from spring to summer. I walk down the stairs and to my car. The parking lot of the apartment complex is weirdly crowded everywhere except the back side of our building. Often, I get the closest spot, which is straight out from the bottom of the steps. It's almost like having my own garage (well, minus the roof… which would be nice during hurricane season).

I head north on Seventeen Business for a couple of miles before turning right into a small neighborhood I've never noticed. It's beautiful. The lots are big, and the houses are even bigger. It's the kind of neighborhood you don't see built anymore. Nowadays, the only question seems to be "how many houses can we fit to maximize profits?" but this neighborhood is quiet and serene. The trees are mature, and though the houses are old, you can tell they've been well maintained.

My phone tells me it's time to turn right and I trust it because, well, that's what I do. The first house on my left is under construction. It looks like they're doubling its size. And then, the next is 1941 Lakeland Drive. When Louise texted me her address, she told me to drive past the front of the house and follow the road as it curves. She said on the side of the house, I would find a circular driveway and I should park in it.

I follow the road and as I turn the corner, I see a woman (who must be Louise) standing in the driveway. I slow down and she must assume I'm her dog walker because she starts waving. I pull in and park my car.

"Good morning," I say as I get out and shut the door.

"Good morning," she replies, looking both tired and relieved.

I take her in. She's a stout woman with a little extra

weight around her midsection. Her white hair is cut short, parting slightly to the left with light curls. Her skin is wrinkled but she does not look like she's nearly seventy-four years old. If I didn't know better, I would guess mid-sixties. She's wearing a light purple three-quarter sleeve cotton shirt and black slacks.

"You must be Emma," she reaches out her hand.

"And you must be Louise," I smile and shake it.

I hear her dog start to bark and look to my right. There are tan, swinging doors, perched between the house and the garage, leading to the backyard. The doors don't reach the ground, leaving an open space, where I see the bottom half of the dog.

"And that must be Daisy?"

"Yes, she's very excited this morning… aren't you, Daisy?" she starts to walk toward the doors and though she doesn't use a cane, she probably should. She takes slow, deliberate steps and I now understand why she can't walk the dog herself.

She pushes open one of the doors. Daisy backs up and lets out a couple more barks.

I follow Louise until the doors swing closed behind me and bend down to greet Daisy.

"Hi puppy," I pet her softly. I have always loved dogs (especially corgis), and she's everything I dreamed she would be. Her back is covered with orangish-brown fur and her belly and paws are white. Her face has a white streak between her eyes that leads to her nose. She's the kind of picture-perfect corgi people must use to design stuffed animals.

Evidently, she is no stranger to attention, because she rolls over and I give her what she wants most: a big, belly rub.

"I'm sorry I kept bothering you last night. I really appreciate you coming. It's been a long week."

"Of course." I'm not sure I mean it, but after seeing Louise, I am glad to help her out… just this once.

I stand up and for the first time I notice the oasis that is the backyard. A brick fence surrounds the space. It's lined with mulch and flowers that look freshly planted. There's a large swimming pool with a diving board and hot tub. The roof extends from the house on the left to make a covered section with four rocking chairs under it. Louise takes a seat in one of them.

"The walk my husband normally takes Daisy on is a little over a half mile. It's basically a block but the roads are a bit funky. If you go out the driveway and take a right, you can follow the road. You'll stay on it until you see Park Street. Take a right on Park, then stay on it and it will change back to Lakeland. You'll make a big circle." She leans down to grab a retractable leash and hands it to me. It has a small pouch attached holding waste bags.

"Please make sure you pick up after Daisy. We like to make sure we keep the neighborhood clean. You can put it in that trash can when you get back." She gestures toward the entry door to the garage where an outdoor trash can sits.

"Of course." I squat down and Daisy comes running toward me. I hook the leash to her collar, and she takes off for the swinging doors, the retractable leash stretching quickly. "Looks like we better get walking," I laugh.

"She's very excited," Louise agrees. "I'll sit out here until you're back and then we can talk about your pay and our schedule going forward."

Schedule? This is a one-time thing.

"Sounds good." It's not necessary to break the bad news to her yet. Although… I thought I already broke it to her on the phone. "We'll be back soon."

I hold the button down on the leash to stop it from extending further and walk out of the backyard. I follow Louise's instructions and take a right out of the driveway.

It's a perfect spring morning. The sky is blue, and the grass is greening up after its dormant winter season. The azaleas are in full-bloom and it's not too hot or cold. I'm wearing black athletic shorts and a lightweight, gray half zip with the words "San Diego" embroidered across the chest. I picked it up as a souvenir a few years ago on a trip to California. Any time I can wear a light sweatshirt and shorts, I'm happy with the weather.

The leash jerks and I stop instinctively. Daisy halted for a potty break. It doesn't require a pickup, so we keep walking.

How am I going to tell her I can't commit to this every day? My internal debate feels like a cartoon with an Angel on one shoulder and the Devil on the other.

(Devil) *It's too much. You have a full-time job and so much going on already.*

(Angel) *Well… you don't really have much going on besides your job. She really needs your help.*

(Devil) *Yeah, right. Who cares about Louise? You just met her anyway.*

(Angel) *She's desperate to get help and you're more than capable. Plus, you could make some extra money.*

(Devil) *Now, the money thing I could get behind!*

Daisy stops again. This time it does require a pickup. She licks my arm as I bend down, and I give her head a few pets. "You're a sweet girl."

We keep walking and the internal debate continues:

(Angel) *You go on walks every morning anyway. Why not help her out?*

(Devil) *This walk is lame compared to the beach.*

(Angel) *It's a beautiful walk.*

(Devil) *Still not the beach.*

(Angel) *Still beautiful.*

I close my eyes and shake my head to try to get them out.

"What are we going to do, Daisy?"

We continue to walk, and I try not to think of anything at all. We make it back to the house much quicker than I expect and I almost miss the turn. Compared to my three-mile walk, this one felt like a blink. Daisy recognizes the house and pulls as hard as she can up the driveway (which is not very hard considering she weighs thirty-five pounds, and her body only sits four inches above the ground).

It takes Louise a second to notice we're back, and she appears slightly startled when she notices.

"How was it?" she asks.

"It was nice." I bend down and unhook Daisy's leash. She runs toward Louise. "Your neighborhood is beautiful." I lift the lid off the trash can and put the waste bag in it. I try not to react at the unbelievable stench that overtakes my nostrils.

"Thank you! It's much bigger than when we first moved in. It's still nice, just busier."

I nod. I'm not trying to make small talk… or get attached. I need to get out of this commitment I didn't think I committed to in the first place.

"Do you want to have a seat?" she gestures toward the rocking chair next to her.

"Sure." What am I doing? Are my brain and mouth not working together? Why do I keep saying things I don't mean? I take a seat and Daisy rubs up against my ankles. I lean down and pet her.

"I know you said you're not available to do this every day–"

Good. At least she heard me. I thought I was going crazy.

"But I'm willing to work with you and make it worth your while. I'll pay you ten dollars per walk. I think that's fair since it takes you about twenty-minutes to do the loop," she adds, talking more to herself than to me. "And you let me know what time of day works and what days of the week you can and can't do. You seem like such a nice girl, and I really need the help."

(Angel) *You can absolutely make it work. She's trying so hard. You know you should help her out. And ten dollars is very generous for what little time it takes you.*

I don't even hear the devil anymore. He knows there's no use. I'm apparently going to be her new dog walker.

"Yeah," I agree. "I'm sure we can work something out."

"Richard is supposed to be able to walk fairly well again after his six-weeks of physical therapy. Although, I'm not convinced he will be able to… but regardless, if you could help me get through that, I'd really appreciate it. Are mornings or afternoons better for you?"

"Mornings. I can't do the afternoons because of my job, and I know you said you're not a morning person but the earlier the better for me. I normally start work at 8:30 a.m."

"You tell me what time and I will make myself a morning person. I can't thank you enough."

She's so sweet. Maybe, this will be good.

"Hmm," I think out loud. "I need to leave here at about 8:10 a.m. to make it home in time to start work. Twenty minutes for the walk. Call it thirty for a bit of a cushion… 7:40 a.m.?"

"Yikes, that's early." Her eyes are wide. "But I can

make that work." She pushes up on the armrests of the rocking chair and arduously stands. "I have to get going to make it to the Inlet. There are limited visiting hours and Richard needs some new clothes. Are you good to come back tomorrow?"

"Yeah, I can do that."

For some reason, I still feel the need to negotiate a little. I can't give in this easily. Yesterday, I said I couldn't do it at all and suddenly, I committed to six-weeks. I stand up from the chair. "I just can't do Saturdays."

"Okay," she nods. "I can find someone to fill in on Saturdays."

I thought negotiating would make me feel better but now I've added more work for her to do and honestly, I feel worse.

"We can take it week by week," I offer a smile. "I might be able to sometimes."

"Perfect." She reaches into her pocket and pulls out a folded ten-dollar bill. She holds it out. "Thank you so much."

"Of course," I grab the money. "Thank you."

"I'll see you tomorrow." She starts toward the back door.

"See you tomorrow."

I offer Daisy a few more pets before turning around and leaving the backyard. I get in my car and put the money in the cup holder. I almost feel like I'm stealing it. Ten dollars for that? It was so easy.

* * *

I'm not surprised Grace isn't up when I get back to our apartment. On the weekends, she doesn't normally rise until ten or eleven, but she said she was planning to check out the new church with me, and the late service is at 11:30 a.m., so she'll likely be up soon.

I walk into my bedroom and turn left immediately into the walk-in closet. It's color-coordinated for no reason other than to be aesthetically pleasing. I barely have enough clothes to fill it, and I essentially wear the same ten outfits on a rotation, so I don't really need them organized for the sake of easy finding. I select a black flowy, spaghetti strap dress patterned with small daisies. It has a rectangular opening on the back, so I wear the tan, lace bralette I bought specifically for under it. It's one of my favorites. I put it on and set the brown sandals I plan to wear off to the side before going to the bathroom to straighten my hair.

My hair is long. Even in a ponytail, it reaches the middle of my back. It's a dirty blonde color now, but by the end of the summer, it will be more of a butter blonde. The sun has always naturally lightened it up. I've never been one to wear a lot of makeup, and before Grace was here, I was back to wearing almost none. But now, since she continues to push me to meet someone, she insists I wear some. To which I always reply, "shouldn't they love me for me?" and she rolls her eyes.

While my straightener heats up, I add some light, sparkly, golden eyeshadow to my eyelids. Grace once told me my eyes were so big, putting eyeshadow on them on was like painting a canvas. My makeup palette shows my desire to keep things consistent, as the gold shade is almost completely worn down, and the other colors barely look touched. I add some mascara to my eyelashes, slightly fill in my eyebrows and evaluate my face. No red spots means I'm going to skip the foundation today and Grace won't be able to say anything. She's always envied my soft, baby-like skin. I try to tell her it's because I don't ever wear anything on it, but she doesn't believe me.

"It's a myth." She always tells me before sharing the same story I've heard more than a dozen times about junior year when she was out of school for two weeks with mono and she didn't wear any makeup and her face looked worse than ever.

I hear Grace's alarm go off in the other room. I carefully straighten my hair and it doesn't take long. Though it's naturally wavy, it's very fine and relatively thin. I'm not sure why I am bothering with straightening it. With the humidity, it will be in a ponytail by noon. I meagerly spray a layer of hairspray before grabbing my sandals on my way out of the bedroom.

Grace is pouring herself a cup of coffee when I get back into the kitchen. Her hair is atop her head in a messy bun. She's still in her pajamas and half of her makeup is done.

"You said we're leaving at 11:15 a.m., right?" she doesn't look up as she stirs coffee cream into her cup.

"Yeah, it says it only takes ten minutes to get there."

"Perfect. I've got plenty of time." She looks up for the first time.

I wait an extra second before obnoxiously asking, "Well, aren't you going to ask me how it went?"

"Oh my gosh! Sorry, I totally forgot. The coffee hasn't kicked in yet, Em." She takes a sip. How was it?"

"You're looking at the newest dog walker in Myrtle Beach." I lift my hands up and shrug my shoulders.

"You're kidding," she erupts in laughter. "Em, you couldn't say 'no?'"

"Grace. You should have seen this woman. She was so helpless and sweet. Her poor husband had this dreadful back surgery, and he won't be home for six-weeks."

"That sucks… what did you sign up for?"

"I'm going to walk her dog every day except Saturdays until her husband is back home. She's going to pay me ten dollars a walk."

"Ten dollars? That's nothing." She scoffs.

"That's a pretty good deal for some people… like myself." I'm used to brushing off her comments. Grace gets paid more than a hundred dollars an hour to do nothing, plus generous bonuses, and commissions on top. I'm not sure why an assistant makes commissions but that's a conversation for another time. She *is* very generous with her money, but sometimes her opinions about it come on a little strong. "Anyway, I already go on walks every morning… so I might as well make a few extra dollars while I do it and help her out."

"True," Grace agrees. "So, if you really think about it… I did you a favor."

I raise an eyebrow at her. "Suuure, you did."

"Well, at least you're getting out in the world and meeting people." She picks up her coffee and moves toward the bathroom. "I've got to finish getting ready but I'm proud of you, Em."

"Thanks, Grace." I dramatically roll my eyes but for some reason, I'm not upset about walking Daisy anymore. In fact… I think I'm looking forward to it.

FIVE

A Trip Down MarshWalk Lane

A week passes and I walk Daisy each morning. I normally get the leash from Louise, make my way around the block, and leave without many words exchanged, but today seems different.

I park in the driveway and hear Daisy start to bark. She now recognizes me and gets excited for our daily walks. Louise is in her usual rocker, reading the newspaper, when I walk into the backyard.

"Good morning," she sets the newspaper down on her lap. "How are you?"

When I see her eyes, I can tell she's tired. She's putting on a smile but it's clear it's taking all her effort. "I'm doing pretty well. You?"

"Tired."

Well, at least I know she's being honest.

Before I can ask any further questions, she continues, "I'm really worried about Richard. I went down to his physical therapy yesterday and I'm just not sure his therapist is doing the best job. The exercises she has him doing don't seem to be smart. She has him squatting and doing things I don't think he should be doing."

Oh really? You don't trust the highly trained physical therapist doing her job? Classic boomer.

"I'm sorry. That doesn't sound good at all," I decide instead to say aloud.

"It's not," she's blunt. I like that about her. "I'm going down there again today to check in with him, but if he's not getting any better, I'm going to call his doctor and have a chat."

"I hope it's better today," I offer hollow words of support. I don't have anything else to give. I know from experience hollow words don't help but I can't think of anything solid. Plus... I still have no interest in getting emotionally attached.

"Me too," she stands and hands me the leash. "I need to finish getting ready. I'm planning to leave soon after you get back."

I get Daisy clipped onto the leash and start toward the road. As I walk, my mind races. Even though I didn't say anything rude aloud, I still feel bothered by my quick reply to Louise's doubts about the doctors and Richard's medical care. I've doubted doctors before. I shouldn't have been so quick to shake off her concerns. In fact, I should have validated them.

After numerous potty stops on our walk, we make it back to Louise's. For such a small dog, I have no idea how Daisy can pee so much.

Louise is outside in her rocker again; this time with her white hair slightly curled and a bit of red lipstick.

"How was the walk?" she asks.

"It was good. Daisy only stopped to pee seven times," I laugh.

She chuckles. "I swear she has to mark her territory in every yard."

"Yes, she does," I agree. I unhook the leash from Daisy's collar and set it on the rocker next to Louise. "How long is the drive to see Richard?" I have no idea why I'm making small talk.

"It's about forty minutes. Richard always drove us places before his surgery, so that's quite the trip for me. I've never been a big fan of driving, but I've been trying to see him at least four days a week. It's getting to be a lot."

"That sounds like a lot," I agree.

"Yeah, it's nice to take him some fresh clothes and some better food. Shockingly, the hospital food is not very good."

Was that sarcasm?

"Shocker." I let out a small laugh, hoping it was. She smiles and I'm thankful I guessed correctly. I've not heard her joke like this before.

"It feels good to laugh. It's so quiet here without Richard."

The thought pains me. Her house is not small, and it must feel incredibly lonely being there by herself. I offer a smile. Again, I don't have words to make it better.

Every time I talk to her, my sympathy grows. I've actively built a mental wall to not become emotionally attached… but it is slowly being taken down brick by brick.

"How long will you stay at the hospital today?"

"Not very long. I have some errands I need to run later, so I can only stay an hour or so."

"Would you want some company? I'd be happy to drive you." The words squeeze out like toothpaste. They're impossible to put back in. What am I doing?

"Oh, that's very nice of you but you don't have to do that."

Here's my chance. I can back out now.

"No, I insist. It's Sunday and I don't have to work. I have no plans and I've been wanting to check out the MarshWalk. It's close to the hospital, isn't it?"

A brick comes tumbling down off the wall and shatters into pieces.

"Well, yes, but –"

"Good. Then, it's settled. I'll drop you off and check it out. Then you won't feel like I'm waiting on you." The words hardly feel like they're coming from my mouth.

"Are you sure? You really don't need to do this. I can handle it myself."

"You'd be doing me a favor. I've lived here over two years now and still haven't found the time to go down. I promise. I'm happy to go."

She hesitates, looking down, silently mulling over the decision.

"Honestly, I would really appreciate it," she finally replies, and when she looks back up, I think I see a tear in her eye.

There goes another brick.

* * *

Ten minutes later, I find myself headed south on Seventeen, driving Louise's Lexus RX, with her riding shotgun. I've never liked driving other people's vehicles. It's always been unnerving to me. Which is yet another bullet point on the confusing list of "why I offered to drive Louise to the hospital."

I've never been great at saying "no." But I didn't even say "no" today. I offered to do something she was never going to ask me to do. I'm not sure what it is about Louise, but I can't help but want to help her. Maybe it's just that she seems so sad and helpless? Or maybe I'm lonelier than I thought? Maybe Grace was right, and any other friend (besides her) is enjoyable company?

"Do you have a boyfriend?" Louise speaks for the first time in the car. She'd spent the first five minutes scrolling through Facebook on her phone. It didn't really bother me, but it *was* the first time I ever felt ignored by an elderly woman on her phone. Normally, I leave that annoyance to be handled by teenagers.

"Uhm," I hesitate, not because I don't know the answer but because the question takes me by surprise. "No, I don't."

"Oh, do you play for the other team?" Louise misreads my hesitation. "I don't judge," she throws up her hands. "I stopped judging a long time ago. It isn't worth my energy."

"No," I suppress a laugh because I know she's being sincere. "I *would* like a boyfriend," I clarify, "I just don't have one."

"Good."

I wait for her to go on, but she doesn't.

"Good?"

"Yeah, that's good. I was worried you'd be taken… a sweet girl like you… but I think I have someone you might like."

Oh great. Another person trying to set me up. Grace will be thrilled.

"Oh yeah?" is all I manage to say aloud.

"Yeah, he's my neighbor's grandson. He's a handsome young man and I know he could use a nice girl. I've known him since he was four. He's a hard worker. I think you guys would get along."

"Nice," I'm at a complete loss for words.

I've only been on one other blind date, and it was a complete flop. I stayed the summer at my aunt's lake house when I was sixteen and she tried to set me up with her best friend's son. He was a nice boy… which is a nice way of saying I didn't find any qualities I liked in him. He was awkward (to say the least) and could have heavily benefited from investing in an acne skincare treatment. The date started with him asking me about my favorite Fortress and Fire character (to which I did not have an answer) and ended with me dodging his bad breath for a goodnight kiss.

"Would you want me to set you up? He lives in the area."

"I'm not so sure."

"I get it. Not into blind dates. Not everyone is and that's okay."

"I'm sure he's a good guy," I quickly add. I don't want her to think I don't appreciate her thoughtfulness, but I'm not interested in a blind date. Plus, I hardly know her. How would she know what kind of guy I like?

"Don't worry," she assures me. "I get it. I just thought I'd offer."

"Thanks."

We ride in silence for a few minutes, though it's not uncomfortable. It's peaceful. The sky is bright blue, and the trees seem especially green today. Of course, there's stop and go traffic on the bypass but still, it's an enjoyable ride.

"Do you have any siblings?" she asks, once again breaking the quietness.

"I have an older brother. He's three years older but we've never been super close."

"Where does he live?"

"He's in D.C. He wants to be some big-shot criminal lawyer or something like that. He was in college when my mom died and he kind of left me and my dad hanging."

"Oh, that's terrible. I'm so sorry to hear about your mother." She sincerely offers.

"It's okay… he didn't like how everything happened and he never could get over it. I guess it's easier for some people to move on and pretend it never happened."

What is it about this woman? I haven't talked about my brother in over a year. I can't believe these words are coming out of my mouth.

"Unfortunately, that is the sad truth."

"That's okay," I want to move on. "Do you have any siblings?" I try to move back to the original topic.

"I had a sister. She was five years older than me, but she passed away two years ago."

"I'm sorry."

"That's okay. Getting old is not for the faint of heart. It's not easy business."

"Doesn't seem like it," I agree.

"I've never had any interest in living forever. I didn't really want to live this long, to be honest… but I guess the big man upstairs had different plans for me, so here I am."

"I don't really care to live forever either," I agree.

"What about your dad? Where is he?"

"He's still living in the Dallas area in the home I grew up in."

"I didn't know you grew up in Texas."

"Yep. Born and raised."

"I've only there been a couple of times, but I really enjoyed it. I went to San Antonio once and Houston the other time."

"Ew… Houston is the armpit of Texas," I laugh. "San Antonio is nice, but I'm partial to Fort Worth."

"I've heard good things about Fort Worth," she agrees.

"It's really fun to see the stockyards and cattle drive, and the food is second to none. Did you grow up here?" I'm doing too much talking. I'd much rather listen.

"No, I grew up in North Carolina. Richard and I met at the University of North Carolina at Chapel Hill. We moved here in 1962."

Mental note: I was negative thirty-five years old.

"It must have been quite a bit different here back then."

"Oh, it was. I can't believe the way Myrtle Beach has been growing, especially in the last five years. When we built our home, there were only thirteen other homes in the neighborhood and well, you see it now. It's crazy. We have a townhouse in North Carolina, and we visit it as often as we can but it's hard to get up there. I much prefer its peacefulness though. It's quiet. It's so loud here." She gestures outside at the considerable number of cars on the road.

"I have to agree with you. The summer is especially ridiculous… but October and November are pure bliss."

"You're right about that. The only time of year it's a slice of heaven."

I nod but don't say anything aloud. Highway Seventeen is getting busier, and the lights are poorly timed. I accelerate when the light turns green and the truck next to me revs its engine and flies ahead to win the race I didn't know we were having.

"Oh, this is a good song," Louise reaches to turn up the radio slightly. "That's the name of the game. I never knew how to play. I was young and dumb, and I never knew what to say," she sings along to the smooth tune.

My stomach turns. It's my mother's favorite song. Or *was*… ugh. I hate the grammar.

"Do you know this song?" she stops singing to ask.

"Yeah," I nearly choke on the word.

"Are you okay?"

I cough. "Yeah, just got something caught in my throat."

"Are you crying?"

"My eyes are just watering from coughing," I lie.

We ride the rest of the way mostly in the quiet, occasionally making small talk about the restaurants and shops we pass. I drop her off at the main entrance of the hospital and head to the MarshWalk. It only takes me three minutes to get there and find a parking spot. I have no idea what I am going to do, but I have always been good at entertaining myself, so I'm confident I can spend an hour wandering around.

I find the wooden boardwalk that runs a half mile in length along the saltwater estuary. It's gorgeous. There are restaurants and shops lining the boardwalk, and a dock where people have berthed their boats to grab a bite to eat and enjoy the waterfront. I stop at the railing to admire the view. The marsh grass is blowing in the wind, and I see a blue heron standing with a fresh catch in its mouth.

Much too early in the day for fish, in my opinion, but to each their own.

My stomach growls, as if to insist it *would* be happy for fish or really anything at the moment. I see a few outdoor tables with people sitting at them up ahead and walk that way.

I get close enough to see the restaurant is named "Dead Dog Saloon," and I am immediately sold. I had a friend once tell me the best restaurants are always ones named with an adjective followed by an animal. I haven't had a bad meal at one.

I walk in, ask for a table outside and get seated right away. It's a nice, spring day; the kind that's almost too cold if the wind blows and you're not in the sun. I take the seat with the best view of the marsh.

"Your server will be right out," she sets the menu down and heads back inside.

I pick it up and start to scan the options.

Breakfast shrimp and grits. Gross. I've come a long way in liking seafood since moving to the beach but shrimp for breakfast? No, thank you.

Biscuits and Gravy. My stomach turns replaying the conversation about my brother with Louise. That's what he would order if he were here.

I continue to survey the options and after deciding, I close the menu and stare out at the water. Normally, I can bury the feelings but today, they feel like they're about to bubble over.

Thankfully, the waitress approaches the table and interrupts my wandering thoughts before they spiral.

"Good morning," she greets. Her voice is thick with the south. She's definitely a born and raised South Carolinian. "What can I get for you, darlin'?"

"I'll take the French toast and a scrambled egg on the side, please."

"You got it. And to drink?"

"Water and coffee."

"Cream and sugar?"

"No, thanks."

"Alrighty," she picks the menu up off the table. "I'll get your order in and those drinks right out to you."

"Thanks."

I hear a cellphone start ringing and I assume it's someone else's. It continues to ring, and I suddenly realize it's coming from my bag. It's never on ringer. The switch must have gotten bumped in my purse. I pick it up and see my dad is calling.

"Hi, Dad," I answer it.

"Hey, Emma Bear. How are you?"

"I'm doing well. You?" it doesn't matter what the

call is about, we always start with this obligatory, depth-less question.

"I'm doing okay."

"Whatcha up to?"

"Nothing much. I just finished my coffee and thought I'd give you a call."

I love my dad, and we have a great relationship, but he almost never just "gives me a call."

"Nice," is all I reply. If I wait long enough, he'll cut to the chase.

"So, I was thinking…"

There it is.

"If you don't have any plans next weekend, would you want to come home? I'd pay for your flight."

"Uhm, let me check," I pull the phone away from my ear and open my calendar. I'm surprised to see next weekend is already March 25. It kind of snuck up on me with everything going on. "I've got nothing. It would be nice to see you."

"Perfect." I can almost hear Dad smiling through the phone. "I thought I would be okay alone this year and I tried not to call you, but I need my girl. I'm really glad you can come."

"You can always call, Dad. You don't have to try to be okay alone," I offer him the same advice he often of-fers me, but neither of us are good at taking it.

"I'll book your flights and send you the info," he ignores my encouragement, but I know this means he heard me.

"Sounds good." The waitress comes back with coffee and ice water and sets it on the table. I move the phone slightly away from my head and mouth, "Thank you."

"Where are you?" he asks.

"I'm out for breakfast."

"Oh, sorry to interrupt. Tell Grace I say 'hi.'"

"It's just me. Grace is still sleeping."

"Oh, what are you doing out alone for breakfast?"

"It's kind of a long story and my food is about to come out," I don't know if this is true or not, but I don't feel like talking. I want to enjoy my coffee and the view. "I'll tell you next weekend."

"Sounds good. Enjoy your breakfast. I can't wait to see you."

"Thanks, Dad. I love you."

"Love you." He hangs up. He never likes to say "bye," for fear of it being the last thing he would ever say to me. I used to think this was kind of silly but now, it means everything to me.

* * *

It's nearly 11:30 a.m. by the time I get back to my apartment. Grace is sitting on the couch, watching the television, when I walk in.

"How was the MarshWalk?" she asks.

I texted her my change of plans during breakfast. Plus, I sent her a picture of my delicious looking French toast and marsh view.

"It was really good. So peaceful. Did you make it to church?"

"No, but I live streamed it."

"Nice," I hang up my purse in the laundry room closet on its designated hook. "Oh, by the way, I'm not going to be here next weekend."

"Where are you going?" she furrows her brows.

"I'm going to stay with my dad for the weekend. It's the twenty-fifth." I don't have to expand; she knows what that means.

"Why didn't you tell me? I can come with you."

"Dad called me while I was at breakfast and said he'd book my flights. You don't have to come."

At this, she stands up and comes toward me. She grabs my shoulders and playfully shakes them. "How many times do I have to tell you? I am here for you. I will always be here for you. I am coming with you. We'll take the jet."

"We don't have to take the jet," I uselessly try to argue but she's already tapping away on her phone.

"Hi, Mr. Rivers."

I throw up my arms. I didn't know she was going to call my dad.

"I'm doing well. Emma was just telling me she's going home next weekend, and you were going to book flights."

I can't hear his response.

"Well, you don't need to do that. I'll have my dad arrange the plane for us." She pauses. "No, really. It's no trouble at all."

I take off my tennis shoes and put them in my closet. Now that Grace is involved, I know I won't need to plan anything else for the trip.

"That's great. We'll see you soon." I hear her say when I walk back. "Okay. Bye bye." She waits a second and hangs up the phone. "There. It's settled."

"Thanks, Grace," I sincerely appreciate her efforts.

"I'll have to talk to my dad, but I think we can head out Thursday night, if you're okay taking Friday off, and come back late Sunday. He normally only uses the plane for business trips Monday through Wednesday, but I'll call him in a bit to check."

"That works. I'm sure I can take the day."

"What about Louise? Can she live without you for the weekend?" she teases.

I shake my head and glare at her. "I don't know why

you're giving me a hard time now… you did this," I chuckle.

"I know, I know." She walks to the candy bowl on the kitchen island and starts unwrapping a fun-size Twix. "You were just supposed to meet a hot, single guy…" she takes a bite, "Not an old lady," she says through a mouth full of chocolate.

SIX

An Unexpected Swim

The week dragged on at an inconceivably slow pace. Grace got our flights scheduled and Louise, of course, said it was fine for me to be gone over the weekend. Since then, I've been anxiously awaiting the trip home.

Louise said she found a young boy in the neighborhood to help walk Daisy occasionally, which makes me feel better about leaving. Even though I've only known her three weeks, the bricks seem to be coming down left and right. I feel a strange sort of responsibility for her. I want her to be taken care of.

She's sitting outside in her usual rocking chair when I arrive. Some mornings, she's inside and I must ring the back doorbell (which, to me, is strange to have a doorbell for your backdoor).

"Good morning."

"Hi, Emma," she looks up from her newspaper. "Do you fly out today?"

"Yes, ma'am. We leave at 6:00 p.m."

"Oh goodness. What time are you going to get to the airport?"

Thankfully, she leaves no room for an answer. I don't feel like explaining the private jet situation to her.

"You'll probably need to be there three hours early. The airport wasn't built for the kind of traffic it gets nowadays."

"Very true," is all I reply. "Hi, Daisy." I squat down and pet Daisy's head. She thanks me with kisses.

"Well, I'll let you get going. I'm sure you have a busy day getting packed up and ready to go. I don't want to keep you."

"Sounds good." I grab the leash off the rocking chair next to her and hook it onto Daisy's collar. It seems like each morning our small talk gets longer and longer, but I do have a lot to do today before we take off, so I am thankful for her consideration.

The spring weather seems to have lasted only for a few weeks and summer is beginning to rear its ugly head. It's humid this morning and I spend the entirety of the walk trying not to sweat. My skin feels sticky underneath my t-shirt and I keep adjusting it, trying to let air blow in to cool it off. I feel a warm drop of sweat trickling down the edge of my right ear, wetting the small wispy hairs, but thankfully, I am only one house away. I can handle a bit of forehead sweat and cool off quickly in the air conditioning of the car on the way home. I hope Louise is still considerate of my time because I do not want to start back sweating. There's nothing worse than sitting in a hot car, with a circle of sweat clinging to your back.

As we turn into the driveway, Daisy unexpectedly lets out a bark and begins to run. Her little legs can hardly move fast enough against the slight friction of the retractable leash.

We enter the backyard and I take off the leash. She bolts around the garage, to the right of the pool.

"Hi, Daisy," I hear an excited voice greet. "Oh, do you want some belly rubs?" the voice changes to a silly, playful tone.

I wasn't expecting anyone but Louise to be here. I've never seen another person at her house, but evidently, Daisy is happy about it.

"Hi, we're back," I announce as I make the turn.

"Hi, Emma," Louise, who had been reaching for the petals of her petunias in a hanging basket, stops and turns toward me. "Oh, have you met Austin before?"

The man, evidently Austin, who had been petting Daisy, looks up for the first time.

His sugar brown eyes look as smooth as honey against the glare of the sun.

"Hi, there," he stands up. It seems like it takes him ages to stretch all the way out. His dark brown hair is longer on the top than it is on the sides and his sideburns help accent his rectangular jaw line. His skin is tanned and already shining with sweat in the early morning heat. "No, I don't believe we've met." He reaches out his hand. "Austin."

"Hi," the word sounds like a whisper I can barely get out. I clear my throat. "Emma."

"It's nice to meet you." He lets go of my hand.

"You too." There go my hopes of not back sweating.

"Austin is my landscaper. I told him my place was really struggling and I needed his help this spring to get it back in working order."

"She says this is struggling," he lightheartedly gestures around the backyard filled with flowers and bushes that appear to be thriving.

"For me it is," Louise argues, "And you should know that. You saw it in its glory days."

"Touché," Austin relents. "My grandparents live next door," he points behind him.

"Ohh," I look at Louise and muster up as much fake surprise in my tone as I'm able. "Do they now?"

"Yeah, but they don't have a pool, so I pretty much spent all my summer days in this one."

I don't respond, instead I turn my gaze to Louise and raise my eyebrows. At least she wasn't wrong about him being handsome.

She shrugs, a sly smirk creeping up at the corners of her mouth. "I needed some help sprucing it up around here." She innocently defends.

"Uh huh. Sure, you did."

Austin looks from Louise to me and back, unsure what to make of the sudden shift in conversation. "I'm going to go walk around the front and see what we can do out there."

He moves toward me, and I step to make room for him to walk. Unfortunately, my foot catches a slightly raised paver and I try to catch my balance but it's too late. Before I know it, I've fallen in the pool.

"Ahh," I shout as I get my head above the water. It's freezing and I'm frantically flailing my arms, trying to find my way out.

My teeth are chattering, and my hands are shaking when I finally make my way to the steps and out of the pool. I suddenly feel the warmth of a towel being wrapped around me and hands rubbing my back and arms.

"Are you okay?" Austin asks. "That water must be freezing."

"Yeeessss," the word slowly spills out through my

trembling teeth. I pull the towel tighter around me. At least I'm not back sweating anymore.

"I'm so sorry," he apologizes. "I should have given you more space and–"

"No," I try to interrupt but my chattering teeth are making it difficult. "It wasn't your fault. I have always been clumsy."

"I'm still so sorry," he insists.

Out of the corner of my eye, I see Louise suppressing a grin. I'm sure she didn't want me to fall in the pool, but I am also sure she's not upset about how this is playing out.

* * *

It's a little after 10:00 a.m. and I'm sitting at the small desk in our apartment that I have come to make my new home office. Its granite top and built in shelves coordinate with the kitchen counters and cabinets. It's not a lot of space but I really don't need a lot of space. I do most of my work on my laptop. Grace is always saying I need to get a second monitor, but I don't mind the smaller, more portable screen. It makes it easy to work from anywhere, even though I never do that… I just like the idea that I *could* work from anywhere *if* I wanted to.

I hear the shower turn off in Grace's bathroom. Her

alarm went off about thirty minutes ago but I've yet to see her today. Since we're leaving tonight, she took the day off to get ready. I'm not sure why she needed the whole day, but then again, what do I know about what it's like to not have to work and have all the money in the world… well, I guess technically, because I'm friends with Grace, I know more than a lot of people, but still, I don't know much.

I get lost in the flyer I'm designing for an upcoming event, and I'm startled when Grace says, "Good Morning."

"Morning," I reply but don't turn around. After twenty minutes of tweaking the same text, it's almost exactly where I want it and I can't risk losing it now. I tap the arrow keys a few more times and finally, I'm pleased with where it's landed on the left side of the page.

"I'm running to get coffee. You want anything?" Grace grabs her keys from the hook by the front door.

My phone vibrates on the desk and distracts me. It's an 843-number I don't have saved. I pick it up and open the text.

(843-555-6267) *Hi Emma. It's Austin.*

"Hello?" Grace asks again, "Do you want anything?"

"Oh, uhm, yeah… I'll take a longboard latte with almond milk please."

"Wait," Grace hurries to my desk. "Who are you texting?"

I hit the power button on my phone and set it down.

"No one," I shrug. "It's for work."

Before I can stop her, she grabs my phone off the desk and unlocks it.

"Who's Austin?!" She exclaims.

"No one… I told you; it's work related."

"Emma. I haven't seen you smile that big at a text since freshman year when you and Danny briefly had a thing. How long are you going to play this game with me?"

I know she's not going to stop until I spill the details. But there really aren't any details to spill.

"I met him this morning. He's Louise's landscaper… see, work related," I explain.

She rolls her eyes at my technicalities. "And now he's just casually texting you?!"

I shrug. "I don't know… you see the extent of the conversation. He said, 'hi,' and I've yet to respond."

"Was he cute?"

"Yeah."

"Was he nice?"

"Yeah."

"Emmaaaaa," she stretches out my name and throws her head back. "Why are you so difficult?"

"Well, it's weird." I finally agree to share a little more. "When I took Louise to the hospital last weekend, she told me she had a nice guy to set me up with and I said I wasn't into blind dates. Then, when I was there this morning, it was clear she facilitated this whole run-in for us to meet."

"And?"

"And what?" I feel like I've made my point.

"And why does that matter? What's wrong with a nice woman wanting to set you up with a nice guy? He's cute and nice and what's the harm? Emma, it's okay to accept help from people every once in a while. You don't have to go it all alone."

I don't have anything to say. She's right. I don't like help.

"You don't think it's weird that Louise just gave him my number?"

"How do you know he didn't ask for it?"

The thought hadn't occurred to me. Could he really have been interested without her pushing it?

"I guess I don't," I admit. "But surely, she did…" I add under my breath.

Grace aggressively hands my phone back to me. "You're impossible." She huffs… "I'm going to go get us coffee."

Just as she opens the front door, the words I was fighting to keep down come bursting out, "What do I say back?"

I can't be certain from the back of her head, but I think she grins. She turns around, successfully suppressing the excitement I know must be there. "Let him wait a few minutes. I'll help you respond when I get back."

"Okay," I agree. I'm trying to not get my hopes up, but it feels like a million butterflies take flight in my stomach. I can't wait to respond.

* * *

It feels like it takes Grace an eternity to get back from getting us coffee, but I know it doesn't. I hear the key twisting in the lock of the door. I stay seated at my desk because I'm trying to play it cool. She's already too excited to help me text Austin back and I don't want to add to her emotions.

"Gosh, it was slammed in there today," she shuts the door with her hip. "Felt like it took forever."

Tell me about it.

"Oh really? I wonder why."

"Spring breakers, I'm sure." She hasn't lived here long but she's seamlessly jumped on the 'locals complaining about tourist season' bandwagon.

"True." I stand up to get my coffee. She set both of our drinks on the kitchen island, and I don't have to check the labels because she got an iced coffee this morning. I grab my cup and take a sip. Yum. It's the perfect temperature for a first drink, although, it's not like it really matters when I'm at home. I'm the kind of person who will sip on a latte for hours (even if it means reheating it ten times).

"I need to get started on some packing." Grace grabs her coffee and walks toward her room.

I don't want to appear too eager, so I just reply, "Sounds good."

I take a seat back at my desk and can't help but feel annoyed at Grace's not fulfilling my unspoken expectations. I wanted her to be excited to help me text Austin back. She's good at this stuff. I'm not.

Ten minutes later, Grace comes storming out of her room.

"What the heck, Em? I thought you wanted my help! Are you already texting Austin back?" she stands in the center of the living room with her arms crossed.

"What? No! I thought you wanted to help me… I was waiting on you!"

"Well… I was waiting on you. I thought you could at least ask for my help." She looks down at the ground, hesitant to make eye contact.

"Grace, you're the one who's been pushing me to meet someone and here I am," I gesture to my phone sitting on the desk, "meeting someone. Of course, I want your help."

Grace has a habit of getting upset if she doesn't explicitly feel needed and I have a tendency to never express my needs. I'm not quite sure how we've remained friends for so long, but sometimes, that very question makes for the best friendships.

She uncrosses her arms, immediately softening her body language. "And I want to help."

"Then what are you waiting for? Come over here and help respond."

She almost skips across the room.

I unlock my phone and open my messages. Grace grabs it out of my hand and begins to pace the room, reading and rereading the message. I'm not sure why we (along with many others of our kind) do this. We analyze and overanalyze until our brains are nearly exploding with possibilities. All he texted was, "Hi Emma. It's Austin," and that's probably all he meant.

But we're left to our own devices and end up examining every option from "he hates me but felt obligated to text because of Louise" to "he wants to run away and get married tomorrow."

Finally, Grace speaks. "I think you should just reply,

'Hi Austin. It was nice to meet you today.' That way, you're being kind and offering a bit more conversation but you're still making him lead it. If he replies, 'you too,' then just forget it. He's not into you. *But*, if he replies with something more, and of course, not desperately quickly," she adds though that wouldn't bother me the same way it would her, "then he's into you."

I shrug and give a slight nod in agreement. The plan sounds as good as any to me.

She hands me the phone and I type out the text that serves as the first test for what (if anything) this could be.

I send it and Grace claps her hands together excitedly.

"I guess we'll just wait and see."

"Yes, we will!" She squeezes my shoulders before heading back to her room. "Let me know the second he texts back! I'm going to keep packing."

"Okay!"

I keep working, trying not to look at the time.

Five minutes pass. Then ten.

I check to see how much time passed between his first text and mine: thirty-one minutes.

I really start to get anxious at thirty-five.

It's over. He's not into me. Why did I even bother getting my hopes up?

My phone vibrates and interrupts my negative, sinking thoughts.

"He texted back," I call before reading it.

"What did he say?" Grace comes running out of the room.

I try to remember the last time I saw Grace run. Was it junior year gym class? No… It must have been racquetball class sophomore year of college. She's more of a yoga and Pilates type, she doesn't care much for cardio.

"What did he say?" she repeats. I unlock my phone and we both read the text.

(Austin) *You too. I know this is a bit forward, but I asked Louise for your number, and I'd like to take you out to dinner. Are you free this weekend?*

"Eek!" Grace squeals with delight. "He's a man who knows what he wants." She nods. "I like him already."

I smile. I don't remember the last time a guy was interested in me and I'm not sure what to say.

"Well, you can't go out this weekend… obviously. But I think that's good. It makes you seem," she pauses and thinks, "not desperate."

I feel like she could have thought longer for a better word but she's not… err… wrong.

"Tell him you're going out of town for the weekend

but you're free the next week." Her tone is dramatic, like it's the best idea of her life.

"I think I could have come up with that one on my own," I tease.

She laughs.

"Let's look him up," Grace pushes my rolling chair out of the way and takes over my computer. "What's his last name?"

"Uhm, I don't know."

"Ugh." She rolls her eyes. "Useless. I will find him."

I ignore her insult.

"Is it Mackie?" she asks, scrolling through profiles and pointing to one.

"Click on it," I instruct. It looks like him, but the picture is too small to be certain. "Yeah, that's him." I can tell for sure when it's full screen. I'm shocked at how quickly she was able to find his profile.

"Oh! He is cute," she exclaims seeing the picture. He's sitting on the beach shirtless with his knees bent and forearms resting on them.

"Yeaaah," I hesitantly reply. "But really… a shirtless pic? What is this 2012?"

"It's not the same," Grace glares. "He's at the beach, casually hanging out… not flexing by himself in some bathroom mirror."

"Touché," I agree.

She continues to click through past profile photos,

of which, he has very few. One from two years ago with a couple of friends, another a few years before that with his grandfather, one from high school prom, another at a football game and his oldest profile picture is a grainy selfie taken in, what looks to be, a fast-food restaurant.

"He looks very sweet," Grace comments. "He's apparently not much for social media though," she scrolls through his wall, "But I think that's a good thing in general… just not good for me stalking him."

I laugh. "He does look nice. Is it too soon to reply?"

"I think you can. He's the one being forward. No need to play *super* hard to get. A little will do."

I type out the text and Grace continues to look online at anything she can find… photos he's tagged in, his about information, possible mutual friends… but, to her dismay, she finds almost nothing. And if Grace can't find anything, no one can.

"Ahh I'm so excited for you, Em!" She nearly yells when she finally surrenders her online search. "I hope it works out. I can't wait to be your Maid of Honor."

"Woah!" I quickly object. "You're moving reaaaally fast there."

"I know," she laughs. "I'm just so happy for you."

She sounds genuine. I can tell she really *is* happy for me… but I'm also guessing she's happy about the timing. She thinks having something fun to think about this weekend will help.

But it won't. Nothing will.

SEVEN

Gone to Texas

"Mr. Rivers!" Grace shouts as she descends the steps off the airplane. "How are you?"

I follow behind her but can't see my dad until she's at the bottom of the staircase. She's a few inches taller than me as it is and when she rides on the plane, she plays the part. She's wearing distressed boyfriend jeans with a white, lace bralette under a black blazer, complete with hot pink, Christian Louboutin pumps. Normally, I play the part with her. She loves to dress me up like her own personal Barbie doll with the latest fashion trends, but not today, I wasn't in the mood. I opted for black jogger pants and a wrinkled, gray t-shirt from college.

"Hi, Grace," he replies and gives her a hug.

"Hi, Dad," I embrace him next. My dad, Peter Rivers, is not a big man. He's no taller than six feet and is exactly what you think of as "averaged size." He has short, espresso colored hair and beige, slightly freckled skin. His black-rimmed glasses magnify his dark blue eyes and constantly slip down the bridge of his nose.

"Hey, Emma Bear," he holds me tight and kisses my cheek before letting go. "How was the flight?"

"Good," I shrug. "It's much easier this way," I gesture to the plane. "You should consider getting one."

He laughs. "I'll think about it."

"You can use the plane anytime," Grace chimes in. "You know that… you just never ask."

"And I never will," Dad grins.

The same man who unloaded Grace's bags in Myrtle Beach unloads our luggage and places it in the back of Dad's dark gray Chevy Malibu. We get into the car, me in the passenger seat and Grace in the middle of the back seat.

"Are you guys hungry?" Dad asks, buckling his seat belt.

"Yes, starved," Grace dramatically replies. "Can we pleaaase get Mexican?"

"Yes, please!" I eagerly agree. "I don't mean to criticize Myrtle Beach, but their Mexican food just does not compare."

"Christina's?" Dad suggests.

"Yes!" We agree in unison.

Give me chips and salsa, along with a sangria swirl margarita, and I'm one happy girl. And Christina's is my favorite. It's a local chain, with a few locations in the north Texas metroplex.

We drive to the Trophy Club location and get seated in a corner booth much too big for the three of us.

My phone dings and I go to silence it. I had it on ringer for meeting up with Dad at the airport and forgot to turn it off.

"Ohh is that Austin?" Grace nosily asks.

"Who's Austin?" Dad quickly adds.

"No and no one," I answer them both.

"It's this guy she's talking to," Grace starts to fill him in. I'm two months older than her and sometimes, she acts like the little sister I never had; unnecessarily telling my dad things he really doesn't need to know.

"Ohh is that so?" he seems genuinely pleased.

"'Talking' is quite the overstatement." I make air quotes. "I met him this morning and we've been texting a little."

"That's nice," he shrugs but doesn't press further.

Does everyone think I'm lonely?

"Hi, welcome to Christina's," the waiter greets as he approaches the table. He puts down a basket of chips and two bowls of salsa. "Can I get you started with something to drink?"

"A strawberry swirl margarita for me please," Grace doesn't hesitate. "On the rocks and sugar on the rim."

"I'll do a frozen sangria swirl with salt on the rim please," I answer when he shifts his gaze to me.

"And a coke for me. Somebody's got to drive," Dad chuckles.

The waiter gives an obligatory laugh to secure his tip. "And can I get you started with any appetizers? Queso? Guacamole?"

Dad looks to us.

"Queso?" I half ask, half suggest.

"Sure," they agree.

"Queso?" the waiter asks to confirm.

"Yeah, that's great." Dad answers.

"Perfect. I'll get that right in for you."

We eat some chips and salsa without speaking words. I find it's necessary to have a moment of silence to enjoy the first few bites of fresh, Texas salsa when it's been far too long since I've last had it.

"I don't really have anything planned for us this weekend," Dad says, breaking the silence. He doesn't need as much time as we do to savor it, considering it's available to him all the time.

"That's okay," I shrug. "It's just nice to be together."

"Thanks for letting me tag along," Grace adds. "Whoa, that was fast." She comments on the tray of drinks approaching our table.

I refrain from drooling over my margarita. It looks delectable.

"Cheers," Dad raises his glass once they've all been set down and the waiter is gone. "To a bad weekend made better with good company."

I bet he was brainstorming that one all week. He loves a good toast. In fact, he'll make us toast to almost everything we eat or drink... ice cream, water, and naturally, his favorite... toast.

"Cheers," we raise our glasses and clink them to his.

* * *

I click off the light and walk across the room. The hardwood floor is cold beneath my bare feet as I make my way to the bed. I pull back the covers and climb in. It's an eerie feeling, being back in a place that once felt so familiar but now feels so far away. That's the thing no one tells you about moving out of your parents' house. It doesn't matter where you go, college, to get a job or across the world, when you come back, you always feel a bit like a stranger.

I adjust the pillow beneath my head and flip onto

my stomach. I wiggle around but it doesn't feel right, so I flip again onto my left side.

A doctor told me one time the best way to sleep is on your left side, supposedly it's better for your heart or something like that. I try to keep my thoughts on better-ing my health. If I focus on that, I can keep my mind from wandering to bigger things.

Thoughts are complicated when you start to think about them (which is a strange thought – thinking about thoughts). Weird.

Wandering thoughts are a lot like spontaneous adventures. On some occasions, you leave the house, ready for whatever may come, and you have the day of a life-time. You hit all the lights green, you see a double rainbow, you eat ice cream sundaes, and everyone is happy. But other days, your adventure goes south. There's traffic on the freeway, you spill hot coffee down your legs, you don't have an umbrella in the pouring rain, and you fight with your family.

Thoughts sometimes wander and end up more like daydreams. They take you to the happiest, best possible outcomes. But other times, like tonight, they find the deepest and darkest places in our minds.

I shouldn't be surprised by the dark thoughts to-night. Most normal people would expect me to be down. But just because something is expected doesn't mean I want it. Like when I'm at a restaurant and really hungry (or rather hangry) and I'm expected to wait until everyone gets their food even though my big, juicy, delicious hamburger is already sitting in front of me. I don't necessarily want to be polite, but it's *expected* of me.

Like tonight, I don't *want* to process my emotions. I don't *want* to think about the dreadful day. I don't *want* any of it. But despite my best efforts, I can't stop the thoughts from rushing in.

Saturday is the seven-year anniversary of my mom's passing. How did it go by so fast? It feels like just yesterday I was a kid, and we were jumping in puddles together after a rainstorm and now, it's been seven years since I last laid eyes on her.

I came home for the weekend to be with my dad. Or at least that's what I tell myself, that *he's* the one who needs *me*. The truth is, I was already contemplating booking a last-minute flight home when he called last Sunday. Every year I think the anniversary will get easier… but it doesn't… it doesn't really get harder either though… I guess it just gets different.

My mother is – well, *was* (ugh… the grammar) – my dad's everything.

She was in her late twenties, working as a Senior Tax Associate at PricewaterhouseCoopers when they met. My dad, a few years older, had already worked his way up to a Tax Manager position. It was love at first sight for them both. They met one day in the cafeteria and the rest was history.

They only dated for eight months before getting engaged and married six months after that. They didn't need a lot of time. They knew it was meant to be. Two years after getting married, they had my older brother, Bennett, and three years after that, they had me.

They were the perfect couple, and we were a picture-perfect family.

Or so that was the mirage I lived. How quickly tragedy can bring down a kingdom.

"Are you asleep?" Grace whispers as she opens the door. I'm not sure why she's bothering to whisper, if I had been asleep, the bright light she's letting stream in would have woken me anyways.

"No."

"Do you mind if I turn the light on? I forgot to lay out my pajamas."

"That's fine."

She flips on the light and tiptoes across the room in her towel the way one does when they're still slightly wet from a shower. She digs through her suitcase and finds her silk pink pajama shorts and a loose-fitting, gray tee. She leaves the room, not bothering to turn the light off or shut the door, which is her passive way of telling me she expects me to stay up until she's ready for bed. It's nothing new. It's been this way for years.

When I was in eighth grade, my parents decided to finish out our attic, and, since my brother was going to be moving out in a year, they gave me first dibs. Of course, I accepted and moved into the gigantic space. They let me design the entire room: the floor, furniture, wall décor… everything.

The room is long, and the ceiling is slanted on both sides. At the end furthest from the door, there's an alcove with a window that looks out to the front yard where I put a white desk. Along the left side of the room, I picked out matching full-size beds with white comforters and pink accent blankets and pillows. At the time, we spent more nights over at Grace's house and I didn't love it. Her home is very formal, and I didn't feel like I could touch anything. I picked out two beds as a lure to spend more nights here and I guess it worked because I don't know if we've spent the night at her house since. The right side has a white dresser that matches the beds, and the wall is covered with a flowery wallpaper I now regret picking.

I look around the room and think about the weekend we spent setting it up. Mom and I pasted the wallpaper while Dad put together the furniture. We blasted music, ate pizza on the floor and relished the adventure of it.

Out of nowhere, this memory crushes me. When Grace walks back into the room, she sees my face and comes to sit next to me on the bed. She wraps her arms around me. I'm a puddle of tears.

* * *

I wake up Saturday morning with a pit in my stomach. I don't want to live the day.

Dad has a few things planned for us to remember Mom and celebrate her life, starting with her favorite breakfast. As I lay in bed, I can smell the bacon sizzling in the kitchen.

What time is it? I roll over and grab my phone. 7:03 a.m. I'm not surprised Dad is already up. He's always up early but I doubt he slept a wink last night.

I quietly grab some clothes and leave the room. Grace is still passed out.

The only bummer of the attic bedroom is the closest bathroom is down the stairs. I brush my teeth, put my contacts in, throw my hair into a messy bun, and get changed before heading to the lower level.

"Good morning," Dad greets. He's wearing his "Hi Hungry. I'm Dad," apron and standing at the island over a countertop skillet filled with bacon.

"Morning," I barely look up as I walk to the coffee maker.

"How did you sleep?" he sounds almost chipper.

"Fine. You?"

"I slept alright. Better than I expected." He opens the refrigerator. "Want a glass of orange juice?" he pulls out a pitcher. "I squeezed it fresh this morning." His tone is overly positive. I know what he's trying to do.

"Dad, don't."

"Don't what?"

"You know."

"Emma Bear, I'm just trying to offer you some orange juice."

"Don't!" I shout suddenly. It comes from deep within me. "Don't try to cheer me up. You can't cheer me up!" Everything I've been pushing down comes barreling out. The same way it did last year… and the year before that… and so the story goes.

I run through the living room and out the sliding glass door to the backyard, shutting it hard behind me. The deck looks out to our big backyard of mostly grass, with a few large trees scattered throughout. I plop down in my favorite cushioned chair and pull my knees in close, burying my head into them.

I hear the sliding door open, but I don't want to look up. I'm embarrassed. I'm sad. I'm angry. I'm so many things and not sure which I want to be the most.

"Emma," Dad's voice is warm and soft, "You can't keep doing this to yourself."

I sigh and breathe in heavily, trying not to choke on my tears.

"But Dad… It's *my* fault Mom is gone. It's all *my* fault. *I'm* the reason we have to live this dreadful day year after year. *I'm* the reason Bennett never talks to us anymore. *I'm* the reason our family is destroyed."

He kneels next to the chair and places his arm around me.

"Emma Bear, that's not true. You have to stop believing that lie. It's not your fault. If you're looking for someone to blame, we know it's not you…" he trails off. "But there's no need to blame anyone. We gain nothing and we change nothing from blaming. You must know it wasn't your fault."

"But Dad…" My chin quivers and my throat tightens. Tears leak in steady streams from the corners of my eyes. "She died thinking I hated her. How can I live with myself?"

Dad stares intently back at me. "She knows you loved her." He squeezes me tighter. "I don't know how to get you to believe that, Emma. She knew you loved her. You can't go on like this. She knew it. I promise."

I'm not sure how long we embrace. It feels like forever, and I never want to let go. In a world where many kids have bad or absent fathers, I hit the dad lottery. If it weren't for him, I don't know how I would be able to go on.

"I love you," he finally says when he lets go.

"I love you, too."

"Should we go eat some breakfast?"

I nod.

"The bacon is probably burned by now."

We both laugh and I feel momentarily lighter after his encouragement. It wasn't my fault. I breath out a long and heavy sigh. I know the weight lifted will be fleeting, so I decide to relish it as long as I'm able.

"I'll take you up on that glass of orange juice now," I smile as I redo my now too messy for my liking messy bun.

"You got it." Dad stands up and I follow him. We walk back into the kitchen. He grabs a juice glass from the cabinet and fills it.

I sit down on one of the stools at the island and he sets the glass in front of me. I take a sip as he starts to scrape off the crispy bacon onto a plate.

"Too crispy?" he asks, examining the bacon.

We both grab a piece and take a bite.

"Actually, it's not too bad," I shrug and grab another.

"Agreed," he does the same.

"So, what's on the menu this morning?" I ask because I know he's excited about it, but I already know the answer.

"Well," he stands up straighter and begins in his best, posh, British cooking show accent, "This morning we are making a brioche French toast topped with a red raspberry sauce, extra, extra crispy bacon, fresh squeezed orange juice, scrambled eggs with cheese and of course, canned cinnamon rolls. All your mother's favorites."

"Sounds absolutely scrumptious," I reply in my own British accent. "But pardon me, kind sir, what on earth are canned cinnamon rolls?"

"Ahh, I'm glad you asked. 'Tis an American classic." He goes to the refrigerator and pulls out a tube. He holds them up with his right hand and gestures below the can with his left. "These are the highly desired and highly delectable canned cinnamon rolls. You could also say they are tubed, but you know, with *the tube* and all, I didn't want us Englishmen, and women, of course, to get confused."

I erupt with laughter, and he joins me. Mom would have loved this. It always seemed the sillier Dad acted, the more she fell in love with him.

I get out several of the ingredients we need and start to help him prepare the French toast. Not long after we put the first few pieces on the skillet, Grace walks into the kitchen. I know she's only up for me. I don't remember the last time I saw her ready for the day before 9:00 a.m.

"Morning," she greets as she walks straight to the coffee maker. "Is this someone's?"

"Oh shoot… I totally forgot about that." I go pick up my cup and head straight for the microwave. There's no way it's still hot.

"It smells delicious down here," she comments as she starts her coffee.

"Thank you! It's almost ready." Dad flips a piece of French toast.

"I guess I woke up at the perfect time."

"That you did!" He agrees.

I pull out the cinnamon rolls and ice them, while Dad puts the finishing touches on the French toast and eggs. We set all the food out on the island in our best arrangement, though Mom would have done it better. I stack my plate with a scoop of eggs, two pieces of French toast, and one cinnamon roll before heading to the dining room. The dining room is around the corner from the kitchen. It holds a wooden farmhouse table big enough for eight and a matching China cabinet, displaying the fine China my parents received from their wedding registry. It really is beautiful, but also, a bit of a waste because they only use it for Christmas. And even at that, we haven't used it at all since Mom died.

On the center of the table, there's a beautiful arrangement I hadn't noticed earlier. It's a vase filled with two dozen yellow roses.

"Those are beautiful," I point to the roses when Dad walks in. "Where did you get them?"

"Believe it or not, I grew them."

"What?" I'm shocked. I always thought my dad was the kind of person who couldn't keep a succulent alive. "Since when are you a gardener?"

"Since last year. I don't exactly have a lot to do these days… so I thought it would be fun to try it out. I'll have to show it to you later… I have a few vegetables planted, though none are producing yet. It's still too early."

"You've been doing this for a year? Why didn't you tell me?"

"I didn't want it to be a flop," he shrugs. "I had a few good vegetables last year, my tomatoes and cucumbers did the best, but it wasn't great. I am hopeful for this year. I learned a lot. I mostly grow vegetables… the only flowers are the roses," he gestures to the vase.

"Wow," Grace sets her plate down on the table. "Those are beautiful!"

"Aren't they? And did you hear he's a gardener now?"

"I did. That's awesome. You'll have to teach me a thing or two… my thumb is black," Grace holds it up.

"Mine too," I agree.

"Hey, mine's like a really, really dark green… it's still in its transition from black," he dodges the compliment.

I take a bite of French toast and talk through it, though I'm not sure why because I hate when other people talk with their mouths full. "I'm excited to see it."

"I thought..." there's hesitation in his voice and he pauses, "I thought you might like to pick some flowers and go to the cemetery with me later." His tone suggests he doesn't know whether he's asking a question or making a statement.

I slowly chew the bite of French toast I'm working on and hold up a finger to indicate I need a moment. I don't need a moment for the food. I need a moment because no fiber of my being wants to go but I also don't want to say "no."

In the few seconds, a million memories race through my head. I think about the day of her burial. I replay every harsh word Bennett said to me. I remember running nowhere and everywhere as I left her grave. I remember it all.

"Dad, I'm sorry, but I don't want to go," I finally say after buying as much time chewing my food as I can. "I'm happy to be here with you for the weekend but that place..." I trail off. He knows what I mean and why I can't go, and he won't make me explain further.

"That's okay," he replies but I can see the hurt in his eyes. He's told me before it's a band aid I just need to rip off. That it's "like riding a horse, the sooner I get back on after being bucked off, the better." But I can't bear the thought of it. I don't want to go.

I've wondered before if I hadn't fought with my brother how I'd feel about going to the cemetery. Would I find peace in it, or would I still hate going? And I truly think I'd hate it. The cemetery, her headstone… it's a physical reminder that she's no longer here. Why do I need a physical, tangible reminder when I have intangible reminders all day every day?

I think about her not being here when I see a mother and daughter sitting together at lunch, and when I smell her favorite flowers, and when I hear her favorite songs, and when I eat a chocolate chip cookie, and when I see a white Honda Accord, and when I *still* pick up my phone to call her and tell her something funny or ask for her advice. I don't *need* to be reminded that she's gone. I *know* she's gone. I see her all around me. I remember her. All. The. Time.

The cemetery is just a sad reminder about the truth I live with every day. A reminder that she's not here and a reminder that it's my fault.

My phone vibrates. I grab it off the table to see that Louise has texted me.

(Louise) *I hope you're having a good weekend in Texas. Enjoy time with your dad. LOL*

Laugh out loud? What's funny about that? I move past it. It's nice of her to text me. She's never sent me anything that wasn't about walking Daisy before.

"Is it Austin?" Grace smirks.

"No, Louise."

She purses her lips, disappointed she can't make further conversation about my "lover/not lover" as she has so kindly decided to refer to him.

I text out a simple "thank you," and put my phone on silent.

"I haven't heard from Austin since we made plans for dinner this Tuesday." I offer up further conversation about him because it's slightly better than talking about the cemetery.

"Ugh. Nothing? It's been two days."

"What are we going to talk about? We don't even know each other."

"That's the pooiint," she dramatically draws out the word. "You text and get to know each other. Then, your first date is less awkward because you already have some material to work with."

"She makes a good point," Dad unexpectedly chimes in.

Does everyone think I'm incapable of having a relationship?

"Well, what do you want me to do about it?" I ask. "Do you want me to text him?"

"Yes! This is the twenty-first century… you can make a move if you want to make a move."

"And I *want* to make a move?"

"Well, don't you?"

I think about it for a second and the answer is "not really," but I know Grace (nor my dad for that matter) will let that answer slide, so instead I say aloud, "I guess."

"Then text him!" She exclaims.

"And say what?"

"Say, 'hey, what's up?'"

"'Hey, what's up?' What is this seventh grade? I can't text that to him!"

"Why not?" Grace protests.

"What's he going to say back? 'Nothin' much. Sup with you?'" I use an exaggerated deep voice.

Grace rolls her eyes. "It's just casual conversation. You could start with something more forward. Like 'Hey, excited for our date on Tuesday. How are you doing?'"

I heavy sigh. "I'm not going to say that either. This is so awkward… can't we just save all the awkwardness for the first date?"

"It's not that awkward. Everyone texts like that these days."

Do they? Do they really? I know Grace is more up to speed on these things but I'm having major middle school flashbacks, and I don't believe her.

"I'm not going to text him. Especially, not today. What am I going to say when he says, 'how's your day going?'" I toss my hands up. "Oh, just dandy. Celebrating the seven-year anniversary of losing my mom. That's a real light conversation starter."

"I'm going to have to switch sides here, Grace." Dad adds and chuckles. "She makes a good point."

"Fine," Grace folds her arms. "All I'm saying is don't come crying to me when you're on your first date and regret not texting him."

"Okie dokie," I smirk. "I won't."

EIGHT

First Date Feelings

The rest of the weekend went by too quickly, the way it always seems to when I'm enjoying myself. We ordered Mom's favorite pizza for dinner on Saturday after Dad got back from the gravesite. Grace probably would have liked to go, but she's too good of a friend to leave me. On Sunday, we went to church and hung out in the afternoon before flying home.

I haven't heard from Austin and, despite numerous further attempts to get me to text first, I also haven't reached out to him. Why should we text? We have a date tomorrow night. We will get to know each other then.

I can't deny the fact that I'm worried he's only taking me out as a favor to Louise. I did kind of expect him to keep the conversation going after we set the date…

but maybe he's just not much of a texter? I won't tell anyone my apprehensions though. I've made my bed about not texting him and I will lie in it.

I pull into Louise's driveway and park in my (now) usual spot. I only skipped two days of walking her, but I'm surprised how much I missed it. In this short time, I've come to enjoy these morning walks. Plus, the extra sixty dollars a week is really helping me keep up with Grace's eating out/coffee habits. The girl can spend money like it's no one's business… but I guess that's what happens when you have too much of it.

I walk through the back gate and am surprised neither Daisy nor Louise is out back. Sometimes, Louise waits inside but I don't know if Daisy has ever been inside when I've arrived. I walk to the backdoor and knock a couple of times. I don't see any lights on inside. I ring the doorbell and hear Daisy erupt with barks.

After a couple more knocks and another doorbell ring, with no sign of movement from within, I opt to call Louise. I have a sinking feeling.

"Hello," her exhausted voice greets from the other end of the line.

"Louise? It's Emma. I'm outside."

"Oh, Emma," she sounds groggy. "What time is it?"

I look at my phone. "7:43 a.m."

"I'm sorry. Give me a couple of minutes. I must have overslept. I'll be right there." She hangs up.

I take a seat in one of the rockers and try not to stress about possibly being late to work. I know it doesn't really matter, and my boss will probably never know, but I don't like to push it. I like my job and it's a good one. I have no desire to lose it.

Even in the shade of the back porch, it feels warm. It's sticky today and I can tell it's going to be a hot one. I can also tell I'm getting older because I talk about the weather far too often.

I hear the backdoor open and stand from the chair. Louise does not look like her normal, kempt self. Her white hair isn't brushed; it's flipping out in some places and matted down in others. Her wrinkled face looks tired with bags under her eyes, and she's wearing a large white t-shirt and gray sweatpants that I assume she slept in.

"I'm so sorry," she starts the moment she steps out from the door. "It was a long weekend and I guess I got used to sleeping in again with a few days without you."

"That's alright. Are you okay?" I feel a bit intrusive asking the question, but I'm worried about her. She looks worn.

"I'm not great," she leans on her cane and takes slow, purposeful steps to her rocker. I sit back down. Once she's seated, she continues, "Richard had an appointment on Friday and his back is not looking great.

There's a lump on it. You can see it clear as day and I had a feeling it was going to be an issue. We went back and forth deciding on which doctor to go with and we went with Tidelands, but we should have gone to Duke."

She continues to ramble, and I don't fully understand half of what she's saying.

"And they think he's going to have to get another surgery to correct the problem."

That I understand. "Another surgery?"

"Yeah, basically the same intensive one he had the first time. The doctor did not do a good job. I think they're going to schedule it for this Friday, and we're going to go to Duke now."

I infer she must be talking about a hospital in North Carolina.

"But he's going to have to be taken in an ambulance. I just worry. One surgery for someone his age is a lot… but two surgeries in six weeks. That's too much."

"I'm sorry. That sounds very stressful."

"It is. And on top of it, I'm fighting our insurance trying to get the in-home care he'll eventually need covered. It's a mess. Getting old is not for the faint of heart."

So you've said. "It doesn't sound like it."

She runs her hand through her disheveled hair. "Sorry, I'm flustered this morning. I was excited to ask you about your trip to Texas, but I was all thrown off with oversleeping. How was it?"

"It was alright. I went because it was the seventh anniversary of my mom's passing, so not the happiest of circumstances. But it was nice to see my dad and be home for a few days."

"I'm glad. I'm sure he was happy to see you."

"Yeah, he was," I agree. I stand up because I need to get going on this walk or I'm really going to be late. "Where's her leash?" Normally, it's sitting on one of the rockers.

"Oh shoot, I left it inside," she starts to stand.

"That's okay. I can get it. Where is it?"

"It should be on the kitchen table. But it's a mess in there. The table hasn't looked that bad in ten years. There's tons of mail and bills and things piled. It's hard for me to keep up. Please don't think it normally looks like that." Her tone is filled with embarrassment.

"No worries at all. I can find it." I walk to the back door and let myself in. I've never seen more than a glimpse inside. To the left is a formal sitting room with blue carpet. Its back wall holds gorgeous built-in shelves with China displayed and it's filled with antique furniture. Though the room is outdated, it must have been stunning in its prime. Straight ahead is an exposed brick wall with a large, stain glass window that gives view to the kitchen. I'm not an architect, but it looks like the formal living room must have been added later because the flow is a bit unconventional. I walk up three steps that lead into the kitchen and see Daisy's leash atop a pile of papers on the table. I figured Louise was exaggerating about the messy table, but she was not. It's completely covered with bills and mail.

There's something intimate about entering someone else's home for the first time… especially, when they aren't there or expecting it. I don't want to linger. I feel bad for her. It's overwhelming. It's quiet and the house feels even bigger inside than it looks from the outside. She must be lonely here without Richard.

I grab the leash and walk out. "Found it."

"Thank you," she sounds genuinely relieved.

"Come here, Daisy," I squat down and hook it onto Daisy's collar. "Let's get walking."

"Have a good walk. I'm going to sit for a bit and then try to get myself more put together than this." She gestures to her clothes and hair. "I should be outside again before you get back, but if I'm not, just ring the doorbell."

I was worried for a split second she'd tell me to let myself in, but I'm thankful she didn't. I am not supposed to be getting attached (though I'm failing miserably). Seeing her house planted another seed of sympathy in my heart, and I'm fairly certain cement is cracking between the bricks of my wall.

We walk around the block and I'm pleasantly surprised Daisy only needed to pee five times. I've decided on average it's two poops and seven pees. I have no idea where this little pup keeps all that waste. On numerous occasions, I've bent down to see if she's really peeing or just pretending to mark her territory. I mean, how can any more possibly come out? But sure enough, she's really been doing it every time.

Louise is sitting out back again when we walk in. Her hair is brushed, and her lips are painted red. She changed into a light purple, three-quarter sleeve cotton shirt (of which I believe she has many colors) and tan pants.

"That was a quick loop today."

Yes, because I'm desperately trying to not be rude but also, not be late to work.

"Yeah, it's a bit warm, so we tried to put a little extra pep in our steps."

"Good," she smiles and holds my gaze. She doesn't say anything, but I can tell she wants to. If I were nicer, I'd ask what's on her mind… or better yet, I'd ask about exactly what I know she's thinking about… but I'm not that nice. So, I bend down, start petting Daisy, and make her decide whether or not she's going to speak.

After a few moments, I assume she must be refraining, so I say, "Well, Daisy, I better get going," and stand to leave.

"Did Austin ever call you?" she finally asks.

I haven't seen her in person since I fell in the pool, and supposedly, Austin asked her for my number that day.

"Ohhh, so we are going to talk about it?" I grin.

"Talk about what?" she deflects. "He happened to be here and then, he asked me for your number."

"Well, that's real convenient coming from the same woman who was trying to set me up with him a mere few days before," I speak in an overly sarcastic tone. We haven't joked around very much before and I want to make sure she knows I'm not being mean.

She smiles and shrugs, "Hmm, I haven't the slightest idea what you're talking about."

I laugh. "Well, then, I haven't the slightest idea what you're talking about." I start to walk toward the gates. I put my hand on one but pause before I push it open. I look back. "We're going out for dinner tomorrow night."

A soft, mischievous smile radiates across Louise's face. "I look forward to hearing about it."

I open the gate and wave my hand but don't look back. "We'll see."

* * *

I repeatedly try to straighten a piece of hair that refuses to cooperate. Austin should be here any minute. Grace picked out a "simple, first date outfit" for me: blue jeans, a black tank too tight for my liking and brown platform sandals. She told me I should be "casual" and "not try too hard."

Although, I'm not sure why she felt the need to pick the outfit for me because I'm the one always being "casual" and not "trying too hard…" it would have come more naturally for me than for her.

"Is *that* how you're wearing your hair?" she sounds appalled.

"What's wrong with it?"

"It's so… so middle schoolish. No one wears a side part like that anymore. It's all about the middle." She grabs my brush and combs my hair back. She carefully parts it down the center and brushes it to the respective sides. "Much better." She commends her work.

I turn around to see my reflection in the mirror. I never thought I'd be able to pull off a middle part but I kind of like it. I look different. Older, maybe? I guess that's why Grace said I looked like a middle-schooler. I've always looked young for my age. Mom always said

I'd be carded until I was thirty and so far, she's been right.

"Don't you agree?"

I realize I haven't said anything aloud since she turned me around. "Yeah, I like–" I almost jump as a knock at the door interrupts me. I don't know what I expected from Austin. I knew he would be here any minute. I guess in this day and age, I thought he'd send me a text when he arrived. I'm surprised (and possibly flattered) by his punctuality and chivalry.

"Is that him?"

"I would assume," I shrug.

"Okay," Grace gives me a once over. "I think you look great," she smiles, and her genuine complement gives me the extra boost of confidence I need to answer the door.

I unlock the deadbolt (which I obsessively lock because we are two, twenty-four-year-old girls living in an apartment with unsecured halls) and open the door.

Austin is smiling. He's even taller than I remembered, and his brown eyes are looking down at me over a small bouquet of wildflowers.

"Hi," he greets.

"Hi," I smile back.

"These are for you," he holds out the flowers.

"Thank you," I'm flattered. The closest thing I've

been given to flowers on a date was an obligatory corsage at high school prom (and he didn't even want to go with me. He was using me to try to get to Grace).

"I picked them myself. There's a field not too far from my house."

"Isn't that illegal?" I mean for it to be light-hearted and a joke, but I am not sure my tone conveys correctly.

"Well, not when you're the landscaper working on the property," he smiles. His wide grin accents his muscular jaw. He's not what I would describe as "my type." He looks more like the kind of guy who would be picking up Grace. He's well-kept, well-mannered, and best of all, handsome. I already know I don't deserve him, and I am quite unsure why he'd want to go out with me… maybe, he just really respects Louise… or he's a serial killer… I'm hoping it's the former.

"They're lovely. Thank you," I sincerely reply.

He's wearing khaki pants and a pale green, linen, buttoned-down shirt paired with brown boat shoes. If I didn't already know it, I'd guess he grew up near the beach. He boasts a natural, seaside ambiance I thought was only reserved for the movies.

"You look beautiful," he compliments.

"Thank you," I reply but don't mean it. I felt more confident about my outfit choice approximately thirty seconds ago. Now, I weirdly can't decide if I feel under-dressed or overdressed… but either way, I don't feel quite right. He looks like he's ready to board a yacht in the Mediterranean and I look like I'm ready for a night out at a college bar.

"You must be Austin," I hear Grace say from behind me.

I'm relieved at her presence. She can lead the conversation for a second while I try to take a deep breath and gear up for the night ahead. I was already nervous, but I didn't remember him being so far out of my league.

"Grace," she reaches out her hand.

"Nice to meet you," he smiles and shakes it.

She lets go and puts her arm around me. "I just want you to know that Emma here is my girl. You better take good care of her."

Oh my gosh. I wanted Grace to talk and now I want to yell at her to stop. She's so embarrassing. First dates are already awkward enough. I don't need my best friend threatening him to start it off.

"Don't worry. I will," he sounds undeniably sincere. "Should we get going?"

"Yeah," I pause, "Wait, I should probably put these in a vase first." I hold up the flowers.

"I can do that for you," Grace reaches to take them from me. "You guys, go. Have fun!"

"Thanks," I'm happy we can go before Grace says anything else to embarrass me. Although, I know I'm being overly sensitive, she's just trying to help. She's *way* too excited for me. Mental note: I need to remind her it's only a first date.

"After you," Austin steps to the side of the doorway and waves his hand. I walk down the steps and wait at the bottom for him to direct me.

"I parked around the corner. I wasn't exactly sure where in the building your apartment would be," he walks a half step ahead of me and leads the way. "I'm the F350."

I'm almost certain that's a truck but I don't know and there are like four trucks in view already. I slow down a step to attempt to not show my hand, but he catches on.

"You have no idea what kind of vehicle that is, do you?" he laughs.

I smile widely and shrug my shoulders in an attempt to flirt. "Nope, not a clue."

"It's a truck," he points two cars ahead. "That black one."

Like a gentleman, he opens the passenger car door for me. I didn't know men like him still existed in the world.

"Thank you." I step up on the foot rail and into the

truck. Although I was feeling underdressed a second ago, I'm now thankful I opted for jeans and not a dress.

He gently closes the door behind me and makes his way to the driver's side.

"Are you still good with Hook and Barrel?"

"Uhm," I hesitate. I'd agreed to the restaurant before looking up the menu, and then I found out how pricey it was and swiftly regretted my agreement. "Are you sure you don't want to go somewhere… uhm… less expensive?" I don't like people spending money on me. Grace is one thing (and even that has taken twenty-plus years of friendship) but a first date at a restaurant with three-dollar signs on Yelp… that's a whole different ballgame and I don't really want to play it.

"Don't worry about it," he coolly replies. "I want to."

I know better than to keep arguing. If he wants to take me there and treat me to a nice dinner, I should let him. I learned a long time ago that by trying to be nice and not accepting someone's gift, you're actually taking the gift away *from* them, and it can do more harm than good.

"Okay," I relent.

He puts the truck in reverse and begins to back out. It feels like a million butterflies have taken flight in my stomach. What if he doesn't take me to the restaurant?

I'm in some stranger's car and I've willingly put myself in this situation. What if he takes me to some abandoned house and–

Don't do that. Don't do that. This is why you shouldn't listen to those stupid, true crime podcasts. That's not going to happen. Louise set us up. He must be a good guy.

"So, how was your trip?" he starts the conversation in a place I wish he hadn't.

"It was alright. I went to see my dad."

"Oh nice. Where is he?"

"North Texas. He's still in the house I grew up in."

"Ahh a Texas girl."

"Yep, born and raised."

"I visited San Antonio once."

I've found everyone always has a story about Texas.

"I loved the River Walk."

"Yeah, it's nice down there. I've only been twice, I think. Did you grow up here?" I desperately want to move on from talk about the weekend. If we get to a third… or maybe fourth date, then I *might* be willing to share about my mom but not tonight.

"Yep. I was born in Murrells Inlet and lived there until I was four. Then, my dad left, and my mom wanted to move closer to her parents. So, we packed up and moved forty minutes north to my grandparents' house."

"That's *much* closer," I offer a laugh.

He smiles and agrees, "Much. Honestly, they did more for me growing up than my mom did. She tried but… let's just say I'm thankful I had them."

I'm surprised. This was not the story I'd pre-written for him. Since we first met at Louise's, I've been trying to guess who he'd be. I figured he grew up in a fancy beach house with two parents who didn't give him much affection but bought him everything. He struck me as the kind of guy who worked because he *wanted* to and not because he *had* to. I never would have guessed he had divorced parents and was half-raised by his grandparents.

Despite his openness, I still don't want to share more about my trip home. I already weirdly open up to Louise. She knocks my brick wall down like it's her job and I don't need someone else like that in my life… at least, not right away.

"Well, I'm glad you had them," I offer, not totally sure what to say.

"Me too. Have you been there?" it's his turn to change the subject. He points out the window to a place called "Blueberry's Grill."

"Yeah, I love that place."

"Me too. It's a good little spot. Maybe we'll have to go there on a second date," he winks.

A second date? We're only five minutes into the first.

"Maybe so," I offer aloud despite my doubts. Surely, after another hour or two with me, he'll wish he hadn't said it.

We pull into the parking lot of Hook and Barrel and walk toward the entrance. The building looks like it's straight out of a South Carolina magazine with its blue siding, white trim and large, wrap around porch. Half of the building is a bakery and bistro called "Croissants" with decadent sweets and savory food, while the other half is the seafood restaurant we're going to. I haven't been to either, though I've heard great things about both.

"Hi," the overly enthusiastic host greets us as we approach the stand outside the doors.

"Hi," Austin replies. "Reservation for Mackie."

"Mackie, huh?" I make general conversation, realizing he never told me his last name. I only found it out due to Grace's impressive detective skills.

"That's my name, don't wear it out," he sings. Before I can reply, he's taking it back. "Oh gosh… that's an embarrassing thing to say. Let's forget I said that," he laughs.

"Oh, I'm never forgetting," I chuckle.

The place isn't crowded, and the reservation isn't

necessary, though I'm impressed he made it. You never know in Myrtle Beach; it could have been an hour and a half wait tonight.

"Right this way," the host grabs a couple of menus and leads us inside the restaurant.

The inside takes me by surprise. It's swanky and modern and doesn't look like anywhere else I've eaten in Myrtle Beach. A large, three-sided bar sits in the center of the room with a light hardwood backdrop and white, specked granite. Beautiful, jellyfish-like light fixtures hang at the center and knotted ropes with one light bulb each hang spaced above the counters. The whole place is the perfect blend of shipwrecked nautical meets fine dining.

He leads us to a table set for four to the right of the bar and Austin pulls out my chair.

"Thank you," I smile and sit down. Austin takes the seat to my right while the host clears the place settings of the other two seats.

"Your server will be right with you," he says as he leaves the table.

"I haven't been here before," I comment. "It's really cool."

"Isn't it? I've only been here a few times and I've yet to be disappointed."

"Good evening," a young, brunette woman nears

the table. "Welcome to Hook and Barrel. Are you two celebrating anything special this evening?"

I feel my cheeks flush. I'm unduly nervous.

"No," Austin casually answers. "Just out for dinner."

"Wonderful," she smiles a much too warm smile at him. "Can I get you started with something to drink?"

Austin politely looks to me to start the ordering.

"I'll take a water to start, please."

"I'll do a water and a Maker's Mark on the rocks."

"You got it. I'll be right back with those."

I make a dramatic face and stick out my tongue. "Blah, I can't do whiskey."

"No? What do you normally drink?"

"Mostly wine," I hum and tilt my head side to side, "And margaritas."

"A tequila girl? Should I be concerned?" he teases.

"No," I laugh. "Despite my taste buds favoring margaritas, I'm about as far from a tequila girl as one can be."

"Oh, is that so?"

"Yeah, I've never really been a partier," I shrug.

"Never?"

"Nope."

"You never had a wild phase? Not college? High school?"

Yet another subject I'd rather avoid tonight. "Nah, I've always been pretty lame. There was a very brief season in high school where I pushed the line but..." I don't know why I'm sharing that. I don't want to think about it. "But other than that, I pretty much live vicariously through Grace's party efforts, and it takes nearly all of *my* effort to take care of her."

He nods and gives a slight, "huh."

"Well, what about you hot shot? Are you a big partier?"

Hot shot? Why did I say that?

"Eh… not really. I think I did more drinking before I was twenty-one than in the years since I turned it. Stupid kid stuff."

"Ah I see. And you're how old now?"

"Twenty-six. And you?"

"Twenty-four."

"And you moved here two years ago?"

I furrow my brows. "Uh, yeah. How did you know that?"

"Oh," he hesitates. "Uhm, Louise told me."

"Oh, did she now?" I chuckle. "And what else did she tell you?"

Austin guiltily bites his lip. "Looks like our drinks are coming." He gestures toward the waitress nearing the table.

"Here's your water and your whiskey." She sets his drink down and flips her hair. I don't know if I'm exaggerating it in my head or not, but she's seemingly throwing herself at him. "Did you decide on anything else?" she looks to me.

I was too busy talking with Austin to further look at drink options. "Hmm," I hum while trying to quickly glance at the menu and pretend she's not giving me a disapproving look. "I'll try the spicy pineapple jalapeño margarita, please." I point to the drink on the menu, as if it's necessary for placing my order.

"Perfect. I'll be back with that margarita and our complimentary pimento cheese platter."

"Thank you."

"So, what do you do for a living?" he asks when she's gone.

"Whoa, not so fast. You don't think I'm going to forget that quickly, do you? What else did Louise tell you about me?"

He grins. "I promise, she didn't tell me much. She told me you were a nice girl, who moved here two years ago. She said you've been walking Daisy while Richard is in the hospital and that you've been a godsend. That's really all I know."

A godsend? That's a little too flattering.

"Really?" I squint my eyes questioning him.

He squints back and then relents, "She did also tell me you were beautiful… and she was right."

My heart flutters. There must be something wrong with him. How is he twenty-six and no one's swooped him up?

"Thank you," I try to genuinely smile. I normally roll my eyes and shrug off compliments but that seems like it would be rude on a first date. There's a brief pause in the conversation and my stomach turns in the silence, trying to think of what to say next. I see the waitress approaching the table again, and I am reminded of two things.

One: Restaurants make for great first dates because they offer a plethora of natural things to talk about. There are the constant table interruptions, the small talk of the taste of food and drinks, the people watching, and of course, if all else fails, you can always look out the window and talk about the weather. That's why I'll never go to a basement restaurant on a first date (well, that, and because I don't want to end up on the next episode of Dateline). Maybe, I'm too paranoid about dating a serial killer. Is that something most people worry about?

Two: I'll never admit it, but a small part of me does wish I'd texted Austin before the date. I'm realizing now there are tons of text-worthy, get-to-know-you questions. You don't have to be looking someone in the eyes for them to tell you their favorite color is blue.

She sets down my margarita and asks, "Have you decided on any appetizers? Or would you like to go ahead and order?"

"Gosh, I don't think we've even looked at our menus," Austin chuckles. "Give us a couple more minutes and I promise, we'll make up our minds."

"Ha ha," she laughs too hard at his comment. "No worries at all," she flirtatiously taps his shoulder. "I'll be back in a few."

Austin picks up his menu and begins to scan. He is either doing a great job pretending not to notice her pleas for his attention or he actually doesn't notice them. Maybe it's the latter and that's why he doesn't have a girl locked down already.

I follow his lead and look at my menu. "What are you thinking?" I ask because I am genuinely curious, but also, because I want to know the appropriate price range to order from. Is he the kind of guy who's planning to order the fresh catch at market price or the cheapest chicken on the menu?

"Hmm, the shrimp and grits look good… or the blackened salmon," he talks and points.

I get my answer: he's very in the middle. I like that. I don't need some guy throwing money around to impress me or one who's going somewhere he really can't afford and stiffing the waitress.

"What about you?"

"I was looking at the shrimp alfredo. I love me some pasta," I obnoxiously smack my lips, and then instantly worry I am embarrassing myself, but he doesn't seem to be bothered.

"Oh, I didn't even see that. That sounds good."

"Yeah," I nod. "That's my final decision. Shrimp alfredo it is."

"I'll go with the shrimp and grits," he sets down his menu. "Otherwise, I might get a little *shellfish* when the meals come." He emphasizes the word.

I put my hands to my face and drop my jaw. "Oh no, oh no," I laugh. "You're a pun guy?" I move my hands from my eyes and see his face beaming with a silly smile. I make my hand into a pretend phone and put it up to my ear. "What's that?" I pause. "Oh, no… okay. I'll be right there." I put the phone down. "So sorry, family emergency. I gotta go."

He erupts with laughter, and I'm tickled. I don't remember the last time I made someone belly laugh with such enthusiasm.

"What can I say?" he shrugs. "I like a good pun."

The waitress walks up to the table, seemingly unamused with our continuing bouts of laughter. I'm guessing she's disappointed with our having a good time.

We order our food and the conversation flows. His

genuine laughter washed away any of my remaining apprehensions.

He tells me his grandfather started a landscaping business forty-five years ago and that he essentially runs it now. He started working for him when he was fifteen, took a break when he went to Clemson for college to study business, and then moved back and has been working there ever since. He's dated a few other girls over the past couple of years but doesn't like to waste his time with anything that isn't serious. His favorite color is green. He's team chocolate over vanilla. He prefers lifting to cardio. His favorite season is fall. And he believes a peach is the most underrated fruit. "It just doesn't get the attention it deserves," according to him.

I have to say I agree. Berries are so overrated. They don't live up to the hype.

After finishing our meals and paying the check, I take note of how much whiskey Austin consumed. I don't like to ride with people who have been drinking.

We walk outside and the sky is dotted with a variety of pinks and oranges as the sun sets.

"Would you want to get some dessert and walk on the beach?" he points to Croissants as we walk by.

"Sure," I smile. "I never turn down cake." I was worried the feelings were only one-sided, but he must be having a good time if he wants the date to continue. Plus, it hardly looked like he touched his drink, but I'm also thankful for more time to pass before driving home. Just in case.

We pick up two pieces of cake to share (red velvet and coconut cream) and park at the eighty-second street public beach entrance. There are a couple of unoccupied benches that overlook the water, and we sit about a foot apart. Austin starts with the red velvet cake, and I start with the coconut. We eat half of our respective slices before switching, and it feels almost too intimate for a first date, sharing food in this way, but I don't mind.

We talk about nothing and everything as the sun goes down behind us and the day becomes night. The beach is one of my favorite places to star gaze. As you stare out, there's nothing to distract from the beauty of the sky and the vastness of the ocean beyond.

"I guess we should probably get going," I say after a while. It's very dark now and I don't want to stay out too late.

Austin checks his watch. "I guess you're right. I can't believe it's almost nine o'clock."

"Time flies when you're having fun," I smile.

His eyes linger on mine for an extra second. Is he going to kiss me? I hold his gaze.

As he starts to lean in, a gust of wind sends the empty to-go containers flying off the bench with a few napkins floating in tow.

"Oh no," he jumps up and chases after the trash in the dark. I don't know how he can see what he's doing but after a few seconds, he's successfully wrangled it all into a messy bundle in both his hands. He walks down the wooden path opposite the water and places it in a trash can.

"Phew," he sighs and dramatically wipes his forehead as he walks back from the trash can. "I think I got it all. Sorry, for the commotion. I hate littering."

"Me too," I say but realize my words don't align with my actions. I literally didn't move an inch to help him.

"Should we get going?" he gestures with his head toward the parking lot.

"I guess so," I stand up and we walk to the truck.

We drive back to the apartment, and he walks me to the door. I try not to think about the fact that Grace is probably standing with her ear on the other side, attempting to listen to our conversation.

"I had a really nice time tonight," his lips curl up in a soft smile.

"I did too," I smile back. His eyes linger again but this time, I can tell he's not going to kiss me. The twinkle that was there at the beach is gone. We stand in silence for a few seconds, and he fidgets with his hands.

"I'll, uh, I'll text you tomorrow."

"Sounds good." I grab the keys out of my purse and unlock the door.

"Have a good night," he offers and turns to go down the stairs.

"You too." I open the door.

Grace is sitting on a barstool at the kitchen island looking at her phone when I walk in. I would bet money she was listening at the door, but I must admit, she's doing a good job of pretending to be casual.

"Sooo, how was it?" she excitedly sets down her phone and looks up.

"It was good."

"Good? That's what you're going to give me?"

"What do you want me to say? It was a first date." I shrug.

"Yeah, but it was *your* first date in like… forevvver. Will there be a second?"

"Maybe."

"Emmmaaa," she only says my name, but I know what she's after.

"I think so."

"Eek! How exciting! Tell me everything."

"I don't know," I shrug again. "What do you want to hear?"

"Ev-er-y-thing," she dramatically enunciates. "Come on, Em!"

"I'm not trying to be short or withhold information… I'm just trying to process it myself first."

"Okay, okay," she finally believes me. "I can't believe he didn't kiss you goodnight…" she adds, almost under her breath.

"Ohh, so you were listening at the door?" I accuse.

"Never said I wasn't," she smirks.

"I think he was about to kiss me when we were at the beach, but then trash blew all over and the moment was lost."

"What do you mean 'trash blew all over'?" Grace raises her eyebrows.

"I guess that does sound pretty ridiculous," I laugh. "We were sitting on a bench at eighty-second street, and we brought cake from Croissants to eat there, and the to-go cartons were empty, and I think he was about to lean in to kiss me and a huge gust of wind sent the containers off the bench and tumbling down the sidewalk. He jumped up to run after them and the napkins that were also blowing, and by the time he got all of them and threw them away, the moment felt lost."

"Oh noo," Grace sticks out her bottom lip to make an exaggerated pouty face. "How sad… that sounds like something out of a Hallmark movie."

"Sounds like a general day in the life of Emma," I retort.

Things like this always seem to happen to me. The awkward. The uncomfortable. It's nothing out of the norm. My personal favorite, "why does this always happen to me moment," is getting the trainee wherever I go. Whether it's a new waiter or a new nurse, if he or she is training, I'll find them.

"Ha ha, touché." Grace laughs.

NINE

A Fight For The Ages

"Good morning," Louise greets from her rocking chair.

"Morning," I smile. Daisy comes running up to me and lets out a soft squeal, like she's trying to play it cool but can't quite contain her excitement. "Hi, Daaaisy," I stretch out her name and squat down to give her belly rubs.

"How was your date?" Louise cuts to the chase. Honestly, I'm not sure if you're supposed to say it or not… I don't think generally grouping all types of people together is allowed these days… *but* I'm gonna say it anyway… I love the way boomers get to the point. They don't mess around with the passive aggressive questions and comments. Louise wants to know how it went, so she asks.

"It was fun. We had a good time." I only spent a few hours with the guy. I don't have much else to say.

"I'm so glad. Do you think there will be a second date?"

"I hope so," the words come tumbling out. I wasn't even that forward about it with Grace.

She smiles but doesn't continue to press. "It's getting hotter out. You can tell the humidity is picking up again. Don't push too hard on your walk and make sure you're staying hydrated."

I want to roll my eyes but instead, I opt for an "I will." She sounds like my mother used to, constantly badgering me to 'keep drinking water' and 'rest.' At least once a summer, I would make the mistake of going out for a walk in the afternoon heat of north Texas and call my mom to come pick me up when I started seeing spots and was much too far away from home.

"Did you get Richard's surgery figured out?"

"Yes," she lets out an exasperated sigh. "Tomorrow night they are going to transport him to Duke. It's about a four-hour drive and they must take him in the ambulance. I am going to have to drive myself. They are taking him late in the night to avoid traffic and get him there for surgery first thing in the morning on Friday. I think I am going to leave tomorrow afternoon, but I haven't decided yet. I have quite a few things I need to get together here before I go but if I could leave today, I'd really like to get ahead."

"Oh gosh. That sounds like a lot. Do you need any help with anything?"

She shrugs. "I'm not sure. I will let you know."

I know she won't. I've been on the receiving end of too many well-intentioned offers to know that an 'I'll let you know,' really means 'thanks but no thanks.' So, I try again more specifically. "Do you need me to take Daisy for a few days?"

"I appreciate the offer, but I am planning to take her with me. We have a nice townhouse not too far from the hospital and some good neighbors up there who will help walk her. Since I'll be staying at the house alone, I wouldn't mind her company."

"That makes sense. Well, let me know if I can help with *anything* before you go." I really want her to know I mean it. "How long will you be in North Carolina?"

"They're hoping for a much faster turnaround this time. They think they'll be able to send him home from the hospital in less than two weeks. At the Inlet, they wanted him in six weeks of physical therapy at the rehabilitation place, but this doctor says he can go home and get some in-home therapy. I think I will go up to our place for four or five days and then come back, but I am going to play it by ear. I might stay longer depending on how he's doing, but I have a lot I have to figure out back here. These insurance companies and their ridiculous policies. We've been paying for long-term care insurance for years and now that we actually need it, they don't want to give us what we've paid for," she huffs.

"I'm sorry. That's frustrating."

"Yeah, it is," she wholeheartedly agrees. "But anyway, I'll let you get out walking before it gets even hotter." She pushes down on the armrests of her rocking chair and slowly stands. "I'll be inside when you get back. I need to get some breakfast."

"Sounds good." I hook Daisy onto her leash and am struck with an idea. "Hey, would you mind if we went on a longer walk this morning? My boss isn't going to be in until the afternoon, and she said I could start late. I'd love to walk Daisy to the water and get her a longer walk in case you end up leaving today and she's cooped up in the car."

"Are you sure? It's so hot today."

We have different versions of "hot." It's seventy degrees and beautiful, in my opinion.

"Yeah, I don't mind at all."

"Well, I have no plans this morning, so if you want to, by all means, enjoy."

"Okay, I think we'll try it out."

She spends the next few minutes explaining how to get to the water from her house in the utmost detail and I don't have the heart to tell her I already know where to go and even if I didn't, I would use my phone. But she finally finishes and we're on our way at last. I'm excited for the long walk ahead and the change in routine. I love walking Daisy, but I do miss my daily walks by the water.

About halfway to the beach, I feel my phone vibrate in the back pocket of my jean shorts and I'm surprised to feel my heart flutter. Am I really that hopeful it's Austin?

I pull the phone out and look at the lock screen. Sure enough, Austin's name pops up with a message notification. I put the phone back in my pocket without reading the message. Play it cool. No need to respond right away.

It's a beautiful day. The sun is shining. I wonder what he said. Did he have a good time? Is he wanting to set up another date?

Emma. Focus. I try to snap myself out of it. I hate how technology has an immense hold on our society. Everyone bonded to each other in a never-ending cycle of communication.

I keep my thoughts away from my phone long enough to make it to the water. It's glimmering against the blue sky. The waves are crashing in perfect rhythm.

And yep, that's it. I've delayed my gratification long enough. I pull out my phone.

(Austin) *Hey Emma. How are you this morning?*

I'm not sure why I was expecting something much more profound, but I am thankful for his casual manner. I guess it's because he didn't text me after setting up our first date that I assumed he wasn't much of a texter… but that was only an assumption. Maybe, he didn't want to waste his time in case he didn't enjoy himself? So, maybe, it's a good thing he's casually texting me now? Hopefully, it means he had a good time.

I put my phone back in my pocket and shake my head. If someone had been watching me over the last minute, they'd probably think I was wild, mumbling to myself and making faces at my phone. Luckily, people have better things to do than watch me walk down the beach.

I don't know why I am getting nervous about texting him back and overthinking everything he says. I guess it's because I like him. Well, I think I like him. I haven't dated very many people before, so I don't want to jump in and commit too quickly. I mean, he still *could* be a serial killer.

A flock of seagulls comes barreling down the beach.

They land ten feet ahead of me and I am grateful for their distraction. They remind me of my mom. She loved birds. She found them to be some of the most majestic creatures, gliding through the air, admiring the world below, or at least, that's what she always assumed they were doing.

Personally, I've never been a fan of birds, but now that she's gone, they remind me of her, and I am always thankful for anything that reminds me of her.

I don't let myself think about the night she died very often. In fact, I actively try to block out every memory of that day and the days and weeks surrounding it, but occasionally, it sneaks in. This morning, I feel my mind tipping back and forth on the balancing scale between Austin and Mom. The crashing waves, sunny skies and pleasant weather are a perfect storm for wandering thoughts. I don't think I'll be able to land on anything surface level with the relaxing peace that is engulfing the world around me.

I let the scale tip slowly to Mom and in an instant, I'm seventeen again.

* * *

I curl the final piece of my blonde hair and it falls to reach the middle of my back. I fluff it up and admire my reflection in the mirror before spraying far too much hairspray to keep it in place. I start to apply some eyeshadow but am interrupted by my mother's voice at the door.

"Hey, you going to be ready to leave in five?"

"For what?" I turn to look at her and furrow my brows.

She pulls her right arm out from behind her back and flashes two tickets in the air. "I got us tickets for Ellie Nova," she beams. "She's playing at American Airlines Center tonight."

All at once, my mind is filled with conflicting thoughts. I told Grace I'd go with her to Dylan's house tonight. His parents are out of town and he's throwing a party. I've never been to a real party before… mostly because I've never been invited to one… of course, Grace is always invited, and she says that means I'm invited too… that "it's assumed" and "we're a package deal," but still, this is different.

Dylan is a senior and we're in the same math class. He's the leading scorer on the football team and the most attractive guy in school. I never thought in a million years he'd notice me… but I guess he did. Yesterday, after class he tapped my shoulder in the hall.

"Hey Emma."

I was shocked to turn around and see him there. I didn't audibly respond, just looked at him.

"I'm having a party at my house tomorrow night. My parents are out of town. I'd love for you to come."

My heart flutters. Did he say he'd *love* for me to come?

"Oh, thanks," I try to respond casually but I'm pretty sure it comes out panicked. "Sounds like a good time." I nervously rub my arm.

"Yeah," he nods and offers a smile. His perfect, white teeth look like they're straight out of a magazine picture. He's the poster child for Texas high school hotties. "Oh, and Grace is welcome to come too, of course," he adds.

I guess we really *are* a package deal.

"Cool. I'll talk to her," I feel the nosey eyes of classmates lingering longer than they should on us chatting and it gives me an extra breath of confidence.

"Awesome. I hope to see you tomorrow," he flashes his smile one last time before throwing his backpack over his shoulder and walking away.

"Are you okay?" Mom's question interrupts the memory. "I thought you'd be excited."

"It's… it's just that…" I stumble, "I already have plans tonight."

"Oh," I can hear the sheer disappointment in her tone. "I didn't realize that. I bought them a few months back when I saw she was coming, and I know how much you love her music. I should have asked if you had plans though."

"Well, I *used* to love her music," I feel the obnoxious need to reply. "She's not exactly cool when you're a junior in high school… more of a middle school thing."

"Oh, well, I still like her," Mom shrugs. She's always been self-assured. She's never cared if her opinion matched other people's. "What are your plans tonight?"

"I'm hanging out with Grace," I reply, which is true… just not the *whole* truth.

"You hang out with Grace all the time," she objects. "Come on, Emma! Ellie is still cool." She grabs my hairbrush off the counter and starts to dance around the bathroom while using it as a microphone. "That's the name of the game. I never knew how to play. I was young and dumb, and I never knew what to say," she sings.

She reaches out, grabs my hand, and tries to spin me around. For a moment, I'm taken back to when everything felt easier. When we'd roll the windows down, blast the music, and sing together on the back roads. I loved listening to Ellie with her. But I snap out of it. My mind flashes to Dylan and his perfect smile.

"No," I yank my hand away. "I'm sorry, but I don't want to." I raise my voice, "That concert is going to be so lame, and I want to hang out with my friends."

"Are you sure?" she calmly asks. She always stays calm, even when I'm not being nice. "You can hang out with Grace anytime… you know we'd have fun," her eyes are soft, she's pleading with me.

I could say "yes." I know we'd have fun, but I don't want to. I *want* to go to the party, and I *want* to kiss Dylan. I can't keep beating around the bush. I have to be serious, or she won't leave me alone.

"Mom! I don't want to go to your stupid, kid concert with you! It's lame and I have plans with friends. Believe it or not, I'm actually kind of becoming popular and that would wreck my reputation. I wouldn't be caught dead at that pre-teen concert with you. So, why don't you just leave me alone and go to your stupid concert by yourself."

Her face drops. I can tell I hit her with a dagger. Suddenly, her demeanor changes. She's cold. "With that attitude, you won't be going anywhere. Not to the concert and most definitely, not to Grace's. You're grounded."

"Mom!" I yell. "Are you kidding me? I'm grounded because what? I don't want to go to your awful concert?"

"No, you're grounded because you're being rude. So, I suggest you make yourself comfortable in your room, because you will not be leaving it this weekend. Give me your phone," she waves her hand out in front of her.

I sigh heavily before picking it up off the counter.

"Ugh," I grunt as I slam it into her hand. I stomp the entire way up the stairs from my bathroom to bedroom and slam the door behind me. "I hate you!" I scream.

I drop down on the floor and throw my head back. I rest it on the edge of my bed and stare up at the ceiling. As if I'm not going to the party. I roll my eyes. I'll wait for her to leave and sneak out the window. Dad will never notice, and I can easily walk to Grace's. It's less than two miles and I'll run if I must… she won't leave for the party for another two hours at least. I have plenty of time.

I replay the conversation with my mom in my head and my anger builds. Ugh. So stupid. I don't *want* to go to her lame concert. I *want* to kiss Dylan. I *will* kiss Dylan and I'll have the time of my life doing it. Who cares if I'm grounded?

I don't know what's gotten into me. I've never been so determined before. I've never even been grounded before… maybe it's the prospect of actually being someone and not just "Grace's friend" or the desire to have my own opinion and freedom. I'm not exactly sure what I'm on at the moment, but I'm going to wring out every last drop of this adrenaline until it's bone dry.

A while later I hear the garage door open and close,

and I know it's Mom leaving. I'm sure she's only going to the concert for the principle of it. She probably doesn't even want to go alone. She only likes Ellie Nova because I do… or did… who am I kidding? I still love her music… it's just that it's lame to like her these days. Everything is lame when you're a junior. Don't like something *too* much or it's lame. Don't work *too* hard or you're a try-hard. Don't care *too* much or you're self-absorbed. So many rules, so little time.

I finally stand up and walk to the door. I slowly crack it open. Thankfully, it doesn't creak. I hear the television on downstairs and am glad Dad's watching something that sounds violent. Much easier to sneak out under the roar of an action scene than a quiet cooking show.

I'm still in my comfortable Saturday clothes: yoga pants and a t-shirt. I make my way over to my closet and pull out the strappy black dress I've been thinking about wearing. It's nothing crazy… spaghetti straps and semi-tightfitting down the middle. It flares out slightly at my hips and falls to my knees. I pair it with white converse, like every high schooler does these days, and toss on a jean jacket. I'm not sure how cool it is outside now that the sun has set.

I place a few pillows under the comforter of my bed. I've never seen a movie where this type of plan actually fools parents, but I figure it's better than nothing.

The window in the alcove of my room sits over the garage. I open it and am suddenly nervous about my plan to get down. The window is small but it's easy to get on the roof from my room… getting down to the ground, on the other hand, is a whole other story.

Five feet down from my window, the shingled roof meets a perpendicular metal roof. The metal roof is about ten feet off the ground. I'll need to slide down the roof and try not to hit the metal too hard. The living room is in the center of the house, so hopefully, even if I make some noise, it won't be loud enough to reach Dad.

I take a deep breath and step out of the window, with my purse hanging across my body. I quietly close the window behind me so that only a tiny gap I can fit my fingers through remains, in case I need to get back in through it later tonight.

The slant of the roof has never looked steep, but sitting on it now, it feels like a slide. I lean back against the roof as far as I can and try to start slowly scootching down it. My shoes lose their grip and all my fears come to life. I slide the last two feet much too fast with a big bang as my butt hits the metal roof.

Oh no. I catch my breath and try to hold it in. I sit as still as I possibly can. Surely, Dad heard me. He had to hear me. A few seconds later, I hear the front door open. The metal roof hangs over the front porch. If dad walks out into the yard, I'm done for. There's no place to hide and he'll most definitely see me. I hold my breath, pull my knees into my chest, and make myself as small as physically possible.

After what feels like ages, I hear the front door shut and I can hardly believe my luck. I have to make it down to the ground without another sound or it's game over. The front right corner of the porch has a white pillar. I think I have enough strength to scooch myself off the side and hold onto it with my legs.

I wait another minute to be sure I am in the clear and then start moving toward the side. I toss my purse off the edge and into the flower bed below. I turn to lay on my stomach and start wiggling myself backwards until my legs hang off the edge. I keep wiggling backwards, little by little until my hips reach the edge as well. I bend my legs down until they kick the pillar.

I know this is a terrible idea. More than that, I know I am not athletic enough to pull it off. Thankfully, the adrenaline is still pumping in my veins, and I decide to go for it. I push myself back a few more times and wrap my legs around the pillar. To my pleasant disbelief, I find myself holding onto it and smoothly sliding down. As soon as my feet hit the mulch, I grab my purse and take off down the road.

There are almost no streetlights in our neighborhood (and I use the word "neighborhood" lightly). We live near the end of a mile-long road with houses along both sides. Each lot is between three and five acres and though it's technically called "The Settlement," I'm not sure most residents could tell you the name. It's really just a country road that's a hidden piece of paradise in a rapidly growing small town.

I switch between jogging and walking down the road. Mostly switching to walking when I'm worried I'm going to break a sweat. There are only two cars that pass and each time, I lay down in the ditch. Our town is too small to risk being spotted by the wrong person. The ditch is deep enough that I am confident they don't see me. However, I am less confident I won't be bitten by a snake… but nevertheless, I make it to the end of the road without any wounds.

More than once on my trek I think about regretting everything from the night, but I force the thoughts out of my mind. All I am thinking about is the party. It's the party of the year. And *I* was invited.

Without much excitement, I cross the main road and continue toward Grace's house. She lives in a gated community on the other, better side of the railroad tracks that run through our small town. The main, farm-to-market road runs north to south, and the railroad runs parallel to it. Although the whole town's average income is much higher than middle-class, west of the tracks is the less expensive side because many of the lots lie alongside the railroad tracks. I am honestly surprised the train horn hasn't blown off the roofs of some of the homes. The tracks are *that* close. Most of the town is on the east side of the tracks. There's more land, bigger houses, and most of all, more money.

I knock on the front door and my cheeks fill with warmth. When I was moving, I couldn't feel the heat quite the same but now that I've stopped, I am about to break a sweat.

Mr. Jones opens the door. He's a tall, broad-shouldered man with dark skin and brown eyes. His hair is coarse and short, barely visible above his scalp. He gives me a questioning glance I'm not used to seeing from his normally warm eyes. He looks beyond me toward the driveway.

"Where's your car?"

"It's in the shop," I'm surprised at how quickly and easily the lie rolls off my tongue. "My mom dropped me off."

"Oh, I would have liked to say 'hello,'" he relaxes a little, though I don't think he totally believes me. "I think Grace is upstairs."

"She's on her way to a concert. She didn't have

much time," I am happy to share some portion of the truth. "I'll go find Grace." I squeeze by him and move into the house. The sprawling ranch is a classic, country style home with dark hardwood floors, wooden pillars, and a plethora of brown shades. I walk through the open concept living room and kitchen. The living room boasts a gorgeous, stone fireplace and the kitchen compliments the color tones with a speckled granite and dark brown cabinets. Off the kitchen, there's a den with a hidden staircase. Upstairs is a media room and a large game room.

I find Grace in the media room scrolling on her phone and half-watching a dating show.

"Hey."

Grace nearly jumps out of her seat. "Oh my gosh! You scared me! What are you doing here?" she grabs a remote, mutes her show, and turns on the lights. "And why do you look so awful?" she turns her nose up when she catches a glimpse of my disheveled hair. Evidently, I did not use enough hairspray.

"I snuck out," I whisper.

Grace dramatically drops her jaw and leaves it there. She stares at me for much too long. "You? You miss goodie little two-shoes. Miss I never ever, ever break the rules. You snuck out?! What? Why on earth did you even need to sneak out?" Grace is genuinely shocked but more than that, she's on the edge of her seat, waiting for the full narrative.

"I got in a fight with my mom, and she grounded me."

Grace stands up and dramatically looks around. "Am I in an alternate reality right now? What in the actual hell is going on? When's the last time you got in a fight with your mom? Me? I get in fights every other day but, you? Have you ever fought with her?"

"Ugh," I throw my hands over my face. "I don't even know what happened. Well, I do… but I don't. She made me so mad. I've been looking forward to this party and she caught me by surprise, and I don't know what I'm doing anymore." I throw myself down onto the couch.

"Dylan's party?" Grace raises her eyebrow. "Are we still going to that? I hear it's going to be super lame."

I sit up and give her my fiercest glare. "Um, yes. Are you kidding me? I just snuck out of the house. I'm going to be in serious trouble and I'm not doing it for nothing. We're going and we're going to have the time of our lives." I can't believe her audacity to suggest we skip it… but, then again, I can. When you're the most popular girl in school, who cares?

"Okay, sorry," she shrugs. "What exactly happened?"

"I was getting ready, and my mom came upstairs to surprise me with tickets to the Ellie Nova concert tonight. I know she was trying to be nice, but I did not want to go. That would be sooo embarrassing."

Grace gives a sympathetic nod and half-smile, indicating she agrees it would be devasting to my already struggling reputation.

"And I told her I had plans with you, and she kept pressing. She wanted me to go so badly, and I didn't want to... Dylan invited me to the party tonight. He invited *me*. And I want to go. I told her I didn't want to go to her stupid concert, and we yelled back and forth until she said I couldn't go anywhere and that I was grounded for my 'bad attitude' and 'being rude.'" I'm talking fast and louder than normal. Replaying the conversation is making me angry again. "And then, she went to the concert anyway and left me at home. So, once she was gone and my dad was distracted, I climbed out of the window and ran here."

"You ran here?"

I'm annoyed this is the one part of the story Grace decided to ask about first.

"Well, I like ran/walked okay... I know... I'm not that athletic," I laugh.

"Goodness, gracious. I don't even know what to say to you," Grace grins a mischievous grin. "I've never been the one on this side before. Usually, you're the sane one in this relationship."

"I really don't know what got into me."

"Do you regret it?"

I bite my lip and shake my head. "I don't think so… I think I kind of… liked it."

"Yes!" Grace shakes my shoulders and raises her arms in the air in victory. "My girl! A rebel!" She celebrates. "We're going to have the night of our lives!"

* * *

"Emma!" I hear my name being called and I snap back to reality. I scan the beach for the source and up ahead, I'm surprised to see Austin running with a dog alongside him.

"Hi," I greet when he's close enough to hear. I'm shocked to see him.

"Who's this?" I squat down to pet the brown and white Border Collie. Her fur is long and soft, and her tongue is hanging out of her mouth, drooling with equal parts exhaustion and satisfaction.

"This is Toffee."

Her name perfectly matchers her coat. To Toffee's dismay, I stop petting her and stand up. Daisy and Toffee take turns sniffing one another before sitting down and enjoying their breaks from walking and running.

"I didn't know you had a dog."

"Yeah, I got her about four years back when she was a puppy to run with me. She's a good one," he gives her an affectionate pet on the head. "What are you doing out here?"

"I decided to walk to the beach today because I had a little extra time."

"You walked from Louise's? That's not a short walk."

"Ehh… I don't mind. I love to be outside."

"Me too," he agrees. "What are the chances we'd run into each other?"

"I have no idea… I guess it must be fate," I offer up like it's some cliché in a romantic comedy, "Like Serendipity."

"Like what?" he raises his eyebrows.

"Serendipity… the movie."

He stares blankly back at me.

"Oh noo. You've never seen Serendipity? John Cusack? Kate Beckinsale? Frozen Hot Chocolate?" I'm pulling out all the stops to jog his memory.

"I have not," he shakes his head.

I throw my hand to my head in a dramatic, disappointed fashion. "I guess I know what we're doing for our next date."

"Oh, so there's going to be another?" his lips turn up slightly into a grin.

Suddenly, I'm embarrassed at my being so presumptuous. "I wouldn't mind another," I try to nonchalantly shrug my shoulders.

"Perfect. Then, it's a date."

* * *

"You'll never guess who we saw on our walk this morning," I announce as I let myself in the back door and find Louise at the kitchen table.

"Who?" she looks up from her stack of papers with genuine curiosity.

"Austin and Toffee." I make the assumption she knows Austin's dog.

"Really? What are the chances?" she smiles. "A fortunate stroke of serendipity if you ask me."

I laugh, "That's exactly what I said, and he'd never seen the movie."

"What?" she looks as appalled as I felt.

"I know," I shake my head. "We're planning to fix that though… I guess there really will be a second date after all."

"Oh good," she grins. "I like you two together."

"First of all, we're not together," I correct. "And

second of all, you better. You're the one who concocted this whole plan in the first place."

She lets out a considerable sigh, "I haven't the faintest idea what you're talking about."

"Mmhmm," I squint my eyes at her. "Let me know when you decide to leave. I'm obviously available to walk Daisy tomorrow if you're still here but otherwise, I'll see you when you get back. Please keep me posted on Richard and your travels. I'll be praying for you guys."

"I really appreciate it," she stands up and for the first time, opens her arms to hug me. I hadn't pegged her as an overly affectionate person, and I'm touched by the gesture. "You've been such a godsend," she whispers as she embraces me. "Thank you."

TEN

A Serendipitous Occasion

It's getting dark as I pull up the driveway to Austin's house. It's a red-brick, ranch style home with a large front porch lined with four white pillars. I'm glad there's still a bit of light left in the day because I've never been to this hidden area of town before, and I might have had trouble finding it after dark.

I grab the bottle of wine I brought off the passenger seat and walk to the front door. He said I didn't need to bring anything, but I don't like to show up empty handed.

"Hi," he opens the storm door and Toffee is right on his heels. I'm not sure if he thinks he's sly about it or not, but he looks me up and down. "You look gorgeous."

My heart flutters at his compliment. It's so genuine and I feel undeserving of it.

"Thank you," I feel my cheeks blush.

"Come in," he takes a step back and gestures for me to enter.

"Hi, Toffee," I bend down and give her some love before taking a look around. I don't know what I was expecting but this place is much bigger than I thought it would be. It's lacking in the interior design realm, filled with mismatched furniture and odd paint choices, but it has good bones.

"I didn't even know this neighborhood was back here."

"Yeah, it's kind of a hidden gem."

"How did you end up here?"

"My grandparents have owned the place forever and they used to use it for short-term rentals. When I was looking for a place of my own, they asked if I'd want to rent it long-term. They gave me a complete steal on the rent, and I think they were happy to have someone who they knew would take care of it and actually pay consistently."

"Oh, that makes sense."

"Yeah, and how could I turn down my own three-bedroom place, fully furnished, and a half mile to the water? It was a no brainer."

Now it all *really* makes sense.

"Yeah, you can't turn that down. That's amazing. How long have you lived here?"

"I moved straight here after graduating from college, sooo," he looks up as he's thinking, "it will be four years this summer."

"Nice," I nod. We've made our way through the living room and into the kitchen while chatting. "I brought this for you," I say as I realize I'm still holding the bottle of wine. I set it on the kitchen counter.

"You didn't need to do that but thank you. Do you want a glass now?"

"No, thanks."

"Are you sure?" he offers again.

"Yeah, I never drink and drive," I state plainly.

"I respect that. I never do either."

What a liar. I furrow my brows. "You literally drove me home after drinking on our first date." The words come out much harsher than I intend.

"No, I didn't," he indignantly replies.

I'm so annoyed. I watched him get whiskey. I don't understand what he's trying to do. My mind races down a rabbit hole faster than I can keep up.

I could leave now. It's only been one date. I don't need to waste my time with a guy I can't trust. What a mistake. How could Louise try to set me up with him?

It's probably been less than a second, but my mind has already left Austin's house ten times in ten different ways.

Suddenly, I take notice of Austin's demeanor and remember his drink barely looking touched. I realize he's not indignant but… embarrassed, maybe?

"I… I…" he starts to stumble. "It seems so stupid now, but I ordered it to try to seem cool. I didn't even take a sip."

I believe him but I don't understand. "You wanted to seem 'cool?'" I make air quotes and raise an eyebrow.

"No… I don't know," he shakes his head, visibly frustrated. "It just seemed easier to order a drink and not drink it than to," he hesitates, "Than to tell a girl I like on our first date that I've been sober for twenty months."

I feel a pit in my stomach. He won't make eye contact with me. Why is it so natural to assume the worst in people?

"I'm sorry. I shouldn't have assumed you would lie."

He won't look up.

"It's a sensitive subject for me too," I reach out my hand and touch his on the counter, trying to make him more comfortable. The feel of his skin on mine relaxes me. I open my mouth to share more, but he gets words out first.

"This is so embarrassing. I'm sorry. Can we just forget it and have a good night?"

"You're embarrassed? You don't even drink and I brought you wine as a gift," I joke, though I am truly embarrassed.

"Oh, come on," he waves his hand and it's only then I realize we've been touching the whole time, "don't worry about that."

I bite my lip, not sure where to go from here.

"So, since you ignored my question the first time, I guess I'll try asking again. Can we just forget it and have a good night?"

"Yes," I grin. "I'd like that." And I *would* like that... I am just not sure I can.

"Great," he smiles a cocky smile.

Somehow, he's both arrogant and unbelievably kind and the two pair together like a great chardonnay and salmon... although, maybe it's not the time for wine similes.

"Did you walk Daisy this morning?"

"No, I haven't walked her since Wednesday. Louise ended up heading to North Carolina early for Richard's surgery and she took her with her. I haven't heard anything about how it went... I think it was scheduled for yesterday morning."

"Oh yeah," Austin sighs. "Gosh, the things those two have been through. My grandma was filling me in on the whole surgery/re-surgery thing yesterday. How awful."

"Yeah," I agree. "I wish I could do more but she's not much for accepting help."

"You're telling me," Austin laughs. "My grandpa offered for years to help her with her landscaping. He'd see her out there almost every summer morning, pruning her flowers, pulling weeds, and occasionally, mowing the lawn. It wasn't until I took over the business, and Richard started going downhill, that she finally relented. She's a tough one… but like she says, 'Getting old is not for the faint of heart.'"

"She's quite the woman," I agree. I want to tell him she reminds me of my mom, but I'm still not ready to talk about it.

Thankfully, he changes the subject. "I picked up popcorn and candy for us. I thought I remembered you saying you prefer chocolate to fruity candies, but I grabbed a bunch of everything… just in case." He grabs a plastic bag off the counter and dumps out a plethora of candy.

"Oh yum! You weren't kidding. And you're right, I do prefer chocolate." I spy an orange package and reach for it. "Can I have the Reese's?"

"Of course. I had my eye on the Kit Kat."

He pops some popcorn and leads me to one of the three bedrooms, which he's turned into a pseudo media room. It has all the potential, and intent, to be a great media room: comfortable seating, large projector, and dark walls, but the taped up, cliché movie posters and blankets tacked up to cover the windows take away from the desired ambiance.

"What?" Austin asks as we move toward the chairs.

"Huh?"

"You laughed."

"No, I didn't."

"Yeah, you did. We walked in the room, you looked around, and then you laughed to yourself."

"What are you talking about?"

"Is it the curtains?"

"You mean the blankets hung with literal tacks on the wall?" I sarcastically reply.

"See," he points an accusing finger at me, "you did laugh."

"Did not."

"It was more of an under your breath chuckle, but still, do you have something to say?" he teases.

"Well… now that you mention it… I think you might, possibly, maybe need some help when it comes to interior design."

"At least you're honest," he lets out a small laugh. "I like you. You're easy to be around."

"Maybe because you haven't been around me too long," I shake off his compliment.

"No, I mean what I said," he genuinely replies.

My insides feel warm. He's so incredibly kind.

There are four reclining chairs divided by cupholders, lined up in one row. I take a seat in one of the middle ones. I'm thankful for the big, reclining chairs that make it easy to pick a seat and not worry about how close I sit to him. If it were a couch, I'd have to worry about sitting close enough that it's not awkward but also, not too close like I'm ready to cuddle the second I sit down. Although, at this point… I think I am.

It makes me smile to see the movie is already up on the screen, ready for him to hit play and start right away. I like the fact that he's prepared and, seemingly, excited for our date.

He takes a seat in the other middle chair next to me and asks if I'm ready to watch while Toffee makes herself comfortable at the base of his chair.

"Yes," I smile. "Are you ready to be dazzled with one of the finest movies of our time?"

"As ready as I'll ever be," he laughs.

About halfway through the movie, after we've both finished our popcorn and candy, I feel my palm begin to sweat. I'm suddenly aware of Austin's arm on the armrest between us and I can think of nothing else. Is he going to hold my hand?

My hands are in my lap, and I notice his arm start

slowly moving toward mine. My pulse quickens and I let my hand find his. His hand feels big around mine, and though it's callused from his years of outdoor work, it's tender and comforting.

As the film plays on, we keep holding hands and I find myself moving closer to him, despite the clunky armrests between us. By the end, my head is on his shoulder, and I want it to stay that way.

"So, what did you think?" I look to him hopefully as the end credits roll.

"I have to admit, it wasn't half-bad."

"Half bad? What are you talking about? It's amazing!"

"It's old… did you see the film quality?"

"Oh my," I roll my eyes. "Who cares about the film quality? It came out in 2001," I laugh. "What did you expect?"

"I'm just saying, I've seen better."

"Okay, then you pick the next movie we watch, and I'll be the judge," I purse my lips.

"Deal."

We lock eyes and I think he's going to kiss me, but Toffee lets out a loud bark and the moment passes.

"You need to go outside? Come on, girl." He gets up from his chair and I follow his lead. We walk through the living room and into the sunroom to let her out the back door. The backyard has large trees that make it a private oasis in busy Myrtle Beach.

"I wonder if we can hear the water tonight," Austin comments and I think he's kidding, but his following silence tells me otherwise.

I stand quietly and listen. Faintly, I can hear the soft crashing of waves.

"Oh wow, I can."

"On nights with no wind and little traffic, you can hear it. Every night, before bed, I come out back and listen for it."

"That's really cool."

We stand in silence for another moment, both looking up at the night sky.

"I should probably get going," I sigh. "I'm not much of a night owl."

"Really? I love the night."

"Yeah, never really been my thing," I shrug.

"I guess that's good news for us… you know what they say, opposites attract."

"Well, then I guess it's good thing you hated my movie," I tease as we make our way to the front door and out onto the porch.

"Hey, now, I never said 'hate.'"

"It's fine, it's fine," I raise my hands. "I get it. I have good taste and you don't."

He chuckles and shakes his head. "I really did have a nice time with you tonight," his tone shifts from teasing to sincere.

"Me too," I let my eyes linger on his.

After a moment, he opens his arms and leans in for a hug. I wrap my arms around him and smell the spicy scent of his cologne. His body feels strong and protective around mine. He runs his fingers through my hair, and I think he's going to kiss me, but instead he shifts his head back and looks at me, "Goodnight, Emma Rivers."

"Goodnight, Austin Mackie."

And with that, I head home, thinking about the events of the night; the feeling of his hand in mine, his vulnerability in sharing a glimpse of his darkest self, the exhilaration of a new relationship and most of all, what it would be like to kiss his handsome lips…

And why they can't be mine.

* * *

"He didn't kiss you again?!" Grace exclaims after I share the details of the night.

"Grace, not everyone kisses everyone on first and second dates."

Even though I agree with her disapproval, I decide

to defend him. Grace always moves too fast in relationships and she's not the one I intend to take all my advice from.

"Sure, they don't," she rolls her eyes. "He needs to get it together or he's going to lose a good one."

"I'm not going to not go out with him because he didn't kiss me on our second date."

"Mmhmm… you say that now… but what about a third or fourth or fifth date with no kiss?"

"I don't know," I shake my head and laugh. "I'll cross that bridge when I get there… and I don't know why you're the one giving me such a hard time. I've been on more dates than you have recently."

"I'm taking a break from men. They're all jerks anyway."

"Ahh so we've made it back to the 'swearing off men for a while' section of the cycle, I see."

"What are you talking about?" she squints her eyes at me.

"You know exactly what I'm talking about."

She blinks rapidly and obnoxiously waves her hand for me to continue.

My notebook is sitting on the coffee table in front of us, so I grab it and a pen, flip it open to a blank page, and start drawing.

Grace's Dating Cycle

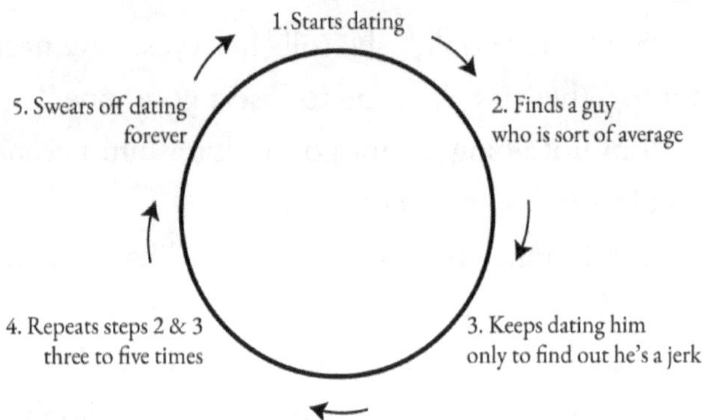

"Oh, that's ridiculous. That's not even true," she denies.

"Really? You don't think?"

"Nope."

"Junior High: Jake, Elias, and Jared. Then, a year hiatus."

"So?"

"High School: Connor, Harry, Kevin, and Jaxson. Then a six-month break before college."

She shrugs her shoulders, so I continue.

"Then, Ford, David —"

"Okaaay," she interrupts. "I get it. Maybe, my ways aren't the best," she throws up her hands, "but I'm just saying… he could kiss you."

We both laugh and relax back into the couch.

"So, what else? Did you talk about anything interesting?"

"We really didn't do a ton of talking tonight. We mostly just watched the movie," I shrug.

"Emma," she shakes her head. "Do you think I can't tell something is bothering you?"

"What are you talking about?" I raise an eyebrow.

"Ohh really? After all that," she waves her hand at the paper I doodled on sitting the coffee table, "you think you're the only one in this relationship who knows the other? No way. You always do this. You're deflecting. What's the hold up?"

"I'm thirsty," I stand up and walk to the kitchen to get a glass of water.

"Deflectiiiing," Grace follows me and leans on the kitchen counter, her eyes unwavering from me.

"What?" I take a sip of water.

"Emma. Come on. What is it?"

I set the cup down and let out an exasperated sigh. "He told me he's been sober for twenty months." I wait for her to react, but she says nothing.

Then I say nothing.

And finally, she prods, "And?"

"And what?"

"And I can't date an alcoholic."

I thought this would be obvious.

"He's not an alcoholic. He's been sober twenty-months," she grins.

"You don't get it!" She hits a soft spot, and she knows it because she stops grinning.

"People change, Emma. Give him the benefit of the doubt. He's twenty-months sober. That's a big deal."

"You're so trusting of everyone. Everyone isn't that great, Grace. Not everything is rainbows and butterflies and —" I stop talking because the tears overtake me.

"It's okay, Emma." She wraps her arms around me and hugs me close.

"I really like him, Grace. I just don't know that I can look past it. I can't be that close to something like that again."

"I know, Em. I know."

ELEVEN

Well… This is Awkward

A week passes and, thankfully, given my busy work week, it was easy to avoid hanging out with Austin. Grace talked me off the ledge of ghosting him forever and encouraged me to give him another chance.

I *want* to give him another chance.

Believe me, I want nothing more than to kiss those lips and learn everything there is to know about him.

I just don't know that it's a safe space for me… and I *need* it to be a safe space.

Begrudgingly, to appease Grace, I've texted him back a bit here and there, and it's been fine.

Scratch that… it's been more than fine.

It's been *great*.

But I can't keep doing it.

I've made up my mind and I can't be involved with someone like him. Someone so close to the worst memories of my past. It's not a good idea. No matter how much I want to… I can't.

Forget Grace's wishes…

I can't keep seeing him.

* * *

Louise got back into town yesterday, after seven days in North Carolina, and asked me if I could make an exception and walk Daisy on Saturday. Of course, I agreed, and I'm actually excited to talk with her again. I haven't even known her two months but I'm comfortable with her. She exudes a peculiar warmness I haven't felt in a lot of years.

I'm up early, and have plenty of time, so I decide to treat myself and pick up a coffee before heading over. Starbucks is on the way, and though I often prefer to buy local, I can't turn down the delicious taste of their caramel macchiato every so often.

I open the door to the coffee shop and on my way to the counter, I hear a familiar voice.

"Well, would you look at this serendipitous occasion."

I look to my right and see Austin sitting at a table

with an elderly man. I feel all the air drain out of my lungs and it takes me a second to respond.

"Oh, hi. I wasn't expecting to see you here."

"I come here every Saturday morning with my grandpa." He gestures to the man across the table from him. "Grandpa meet Emma and Emma meet Grandpa."

His grandfather, with a thick head of light gray hair, looks up from his brown-rimmed glasses, and reaches out his hand. "Oh, what a lovely surprise to meet the girl Austin's been talking about nonstop."

"Grandpa," he chides. His cheeks flush with embarrassment.

"The pleasure is mine," I shake his hand. "I've heard nothing but the best things about you and your wife from Austin and Louise."

"Oh, that's right. You're the one who's been walking Daisy."

"That's me." I nod. "I'm actually on my way there right now. Just thought I'd pick up a little caffeine this morning."

"Well, we won't keep you," Austin quickly replies. It's clear he doesn't want to give his grandfather time to say anything else he might find humiliating.

"Okay," I'm relieved. "It was nice to meet you."

"You too," his grandpa replies.

I start to walk toward the counter and when I'm a

few steps away from the table, I hear their murmuring conversation.

"Well, aren't you going to buy her a drink?"

"I'm not even here with her."

"You could still be a gentleman."

I don't turn around; out of fear they'd know I heard their attempt at whispering and continue to the counter.

As I finish ordering, I feel a hand gently touch the center of my back.

"This one's on me," Austin tells the barista after she rings it up.

"You don't have to do that."

"I'm happy to… in the spirit of serendipity."

"You seem to be really into this serendipity thing for a guy who didn't much care for the movie," I tease. We walk to the other end of the counter to wait for my drink.

He shrugs. "I was going to text you today. I wanted to see if you'd be up for dinner tonight?"

I wish he had texted me. Then, I would have had time to write a tactful response and say no. I could have hidden behind my phone and planned to never see him again.

But I hate disappointing people and he's looking at me like a helpless puppy dog, so, of course, I say, "Yeah, that sounds great."

"Perfect," he beams.

"Emma," the barista calls and sets down my drink.

"I know you need to get going. I'll text you about plans."

"Sounds good," I feign a smile.

* * *

The temperature is pleasant due to last night's rain, and the broken humidity, as I rock and chat with Louise. I already walked Daisy around the loop, and I have nothing to do today (or rather I *had* nothing to do).

I can tell she's in the mood to talk and I'm in the mood to not think about my own problems, so I settle in and listen.

"Well, I think Richard is doing better. The surgery was much more successful this time around and I liked this doctor's attitude a lot more. I wish we had gone to Duke in the first place… but the past is the past. Can't change it."

"I'm glad he's doing better."

"Me too. I think he should be coming home later this week."

"Really? Like home home?"

"Yeah, he'll be here. I'm trying to get a nurse to come to the house daily, which of course, is a struggle. But I'll be glad to have him back."

"Oh, wow. Yeah, that's much faster than last time. I'm so happy to hear that." And I really am. I've thought more than once about how lonely it must be for Louise to be in this big house without him. It's really no surprise she pays me too much money to walk Daisy and keep her company.

"But enough about me. How have you been? I haven't seen Austin lately. He must be too busy wooing you."

Wooing? I suppress a laugh. I love Louise's vocabulary.

"We've been alright." I keep it surface level in hopes we can move on to a different subject.

"Has he kissed you yet?"

I wish I could say I'm shocked at her question but I'm not. She's incredibly blunt.

"No, not yet," I half frown but I'm not sure why. My emotions are too conflicting to sort out at the moment.

"Why am I not surprised? That boy moves slower than molasses. But I tell you what… I bet it's a good thing. He's a careful one. It probably means he doesn't want to mess it up."

"You think?"

"I do. I've only ever seen him date one or two other girls his whole life. He's not been much for dating, given the nature of his parents."

"Makes sense," I comment like I know what she's talking about, but I don't really. I assume it's because he doesn't want to deal with divorce or commitment. I know his dad left when he was young, he told me that on our first date, but since then, the topic of parents hasn't really come up again. Maybe, we're both purposefully avoiding it.

"His mom," she disappointedly shakes her head. "I don't know how someone that messed up came out of a house with those two wonderful people next door."

I almost feel like I'm intruding, hearing this from Louise and not Austin.

"I actually met his grandpa this morning. He's a very nice man," I try to shift the conversation but either she doesn't hear me, or she doesn't care.

"She's been in and out of prison the last few years... struggled with drug addictions and alcohol abuse. It's dreadful."

"That's terrible. I guess it makes sense Austin would have struggled a bit with it too," I can't catch the words before they're falling out of my mouth. I don't understand why I'm such an open book when it comes to Louise. I don't normally have an issue holding my tongue.

"What on earth are you talking about?" Louise knits her brows.

Oh no. Maybe she doesn't know about his struggles. I bite my lip and decide my toes are already in my mouth… I might as well put my whole foot in there. "He told me he's been sober for the last twenty months."

"And?"

"And what? He made it sound like he had a problem with alcohol before that."

She laughs.

I'm confused.

"Do you always assume the worst in people?"

"No," I quickly defend.

"Austin's never had a problem with drinking," she shakes it off like it's the most absurd information she's ever heard. "I know he tends to stop drinking when his mom is doing really poorly, but he's never been an addict himself."

"Why would he tell me he's been sober twenty months then?"

"I know his mother isn't doing well right now. He probably hasn't been drinking since she went off the grid again. I don't know the context of the conversation, but that's my best guess. He probably didn't want to get into the nitty gritty of it all. I mean… can you blame him? It was probably easier for him to say that, rather than explain all his childhood traumas."

My mind is spinning. I fought with myself all week

about getting involved with a guy who has a history with alcohol… given *my* history. But now… if this is true… if my biggest issue isn't his past but instead his present inability to kiss me… well, then, that's hardly a problem at all.

My phone vibrates in the front pocket of my jeans, and I don't have to look to know who texted me.

I guess now I know what we'll be talking about at dinner tonight. And I'm looking forward to it.

* * *

Austin picks me up a little before six o'clock and we head to Fiesta Mexicana. It's the only good Mexican restaurant in town, in my humble opinion.

He looks handsome in his casual clothes and I'm not upset that his jeans are a tighter fit. I can't deny that I am pleased to be able to look at him with fresh eyes again.

I really hope Louise is right.

We grab a table outside. There's a slight chill in the air, with the sun going down, which is probably why the patio is nearly empty, but I think we'll still be warm enough.

I spent the afternoon talking through numerous scenarios with Grace: how to bring it up, what if it is true and Louise is wrong, what about my past, how much should I share?

An afternoon of planning evidently wasted because as I sit down and make eye contact with him, I'm once again lost in his dazzling brown eyes, and I can't remember a thing we decided.

"I'm so glad you could do dinner tonight. I know we haven't texted much this week, but it was a bit crazy with work and everything. I really did have a great time last weekend and I'm excited to hang out again."

"Me too," is all I get out before the waiter approaches our table with chips and salsa.

"What can I get you guys to drink?"

"Just water for me please," I order.

"Me too."

Should I bring it up? It seems like a natural time with the ordering of drinks. Before I can, he's talking.

"Sorry about my grandpa this morning. He's quite a hoot."

"Oh, no worries at all. He seems like a really nice guy…" I hesitate, "Though I do have to admit, I *did* hear him telling you to buy my drink."

"I figured," he shakes his head. "He's eighty-seven and still does pretty well. He's fit and has his mind, but his hearing… he's been losing that for years now. I'm pretty sure the whole place heard us this morning."

We both laugh and fall quiet. I seize the moment to start talking. I want the debate in my mind to end.

"Hey, listen. I've been struggling all week and I really need to ask you something." I'm trying to build up my courage as I go. I know now, looking into his eyes, that I have to ask, or I never will. He's too handsome. I can't waste my time thinking about his lips on mine if it can never happen. I need to know now, or I need to go.

"What is it?" he looks seriously back at me.

In a moment, all the diplomatic ways I could phrase the question flash though my head and instead, I land on, "Were you an alcoholic?"

"What?" he flatly questions.

The waiter delivers our waters to the table at the most inconvenient time.

"Are you guys ready to order?"
"We'll need another minute," Austin courteously replies, though I know he doesn't feel as calm as he appears. When the waiter is gone, he looks back to me.
"Am I an alcoholic?"

It doesn't feel like the right time to correct him but *did* ask if he *was* an alcoholic, not if he *is*.

"Why are you so surprised by the question? You told me last weekend you've been sober for twenty-months."

"Yeah, so?"
"So? What do you mean, 'so?'"

"So, what if I've been sober?"

"I'm beyond confused here. Sober means you were addicted and then you stopped and then you've gone however long post-addiction without drinking."

"Technically, it just means you're not drinking alcohol and that's true. I haven't had any in the past twenty-months."

I feel like I'm really losing hold of this conversation. I put my hands to my temples and close my eyes for a second.

"Okay," I finally breath out. "So, you've never been an alcoholic then?" I try to summarize.

"Correct. I have never been addicted to alcohol."

"Well, that's good news," is all I can say. I don't really know if I want to laugh or cry or yell.

The waiter comes back to the table, and we place our orders. This time, I am thankful for his timing.

"I'm sorry. I'm parrying," Austin starts when the waiter is gone again. "I knew this would have to come up eventually if we kept talking but… it's painful."

I wait for him to keep going and try to greet him with soft, accepting eyes. If there's one thing I know for certain, it's pain.

"My mom is… I really do love her but… she's not a great person. She makes a lot of mistakes, and her biggest ones often involve alcohol. I'm still learning to deal with it and process it and everything. I don't know why I pretended to drink whiskey on our first date or use the terminology 'sober' on our second. Alcohol is a strange subject, you know? For some people it's so casual, so uninhibited, so senseless," he sighs heavily, "But it's just not that way for me and I think I've been nervous. The truth is I really like you. You're smart and kind and beautiful. When I first laid eyes on you at Louise's, I knew I didn't want to mess anything up and now I'm rambling and –" he rubs his hand on his forehead, "I don't know. I'm sorry," he offers the apology again.

"It's okay," I reach my hand out across the table and am glad when he grabs hold of it. It's warm and soft in mine. "It's not easy for me either," I assure him.

"You don't have to say that to make me feel better."

"I promise, I'm not," I take a deep breath. "My mom died when I was seventeen… she was hit by a drunk driver. Which is why I don't get in the car with someone who has been drinking."

"I'm… I'm so sorry," he stumbles over his words the same way most people do when they hear about her death for the first time. "That's awful."

"Yeah," I shrug. "It was. And is."

"Can I ask a question though?"

"Of course."

"If you don't get in the car with people who have

been drinking, then why did you let me drive you home on our first date?"

"I took careful note of how much was left in your drink. It didn't even look like you'd touched it. I figured you were distracted with talking and forgot about it."

"Oh," he nods in approval. "That makes sense."

"Yeah… I also didn't want to get into all of it and my rules an hour into meeting you… so don't think you're the only one who has a weird relationship with alcohol here," I point between the two of us. "You can't just claim that one, buddy boy," I laugh.

"Buddy boy?" he raises an eyebrow.

"I meant what I said."

"Okay, okay," he raises his hands in surrender. "You're right. I prematurely made the claim. We can share the title." He joins in my laughter and my heart is full of relief.

"What a lovely title to share," I smile and flirtatiously roll my eyes.

We sigh at the same time and the invisible tension seems to be cut.

"So… where's your mom now?" I ask and then quickly add, "I mean, if you don't mind me asking."

"Not at all," he replies. "I think she's currently in a rehabilitation center somewhere in North Carolina, but I haven't heard from her in… well… twenty-months. I think it was a bust for cocaine this time, but I really don't know."

"I'm so sorry. That must be really difficult."

"It has been at times. I'm grateful for my grandparents though. Without them, I am not sure where I'd be."

"I'm glad you have them," I agree. "That's special."

And it really is… because thanks to them, I am sitting across from someone who is kind, intelligent and successful against all odds. Someone whom I might actually be falling for.

* * *

I walk in the door to the apartment and cannot hide the smile beaming across my face. Grace runs out of her bedroom and immediately, she knows.

"He finally kissed you?!" her eyes are illuminated with excitement.

"He did," I sigh happily.

"Ahh," she throws up her hands. "That must mean things went well. Tell me everything. Come here and tell me everything right now," she plops down on the couch and feverishly taps the seat next to her.

I take my purse off of my shoulder and set it on the kitchen counter. I slowly walk to the couch. I want to talk to Grace, but I also want to process everything myself. "I don't even know where to start," I say as I take a seat.

"Start with the kiss! You *have* to start with the kiss."

Grace makes me laugh. She has more enthusiasm than anyone I know.

"Well, there's not too much to tell. When we got back here after dinner, we got out of the car and he started walking me to our door. We kind of naturally stopped near the bottom of the steps and continued chatting for a bit. Then, he asked me if it would be alright if he kissed me and I said, 'yes,' and then he leaned in."

"Ahhhh," Grace squeals. "I love new love. He seems like such a gentleman. How was the kiss? Is he a good kisser?"

I shake my head and laugh. "Grace, it was hardly more than a peck and I haven't kissed a guy in probably four years. So, yeah, it was a nice kiss."

"Oh, I am SO happy!" She's nearly shouting. "And what was the deal with the alcohol thing? Was Louise right? How did it come up?"

"Yeah, she was. He's never been an alcoholic and his mom definitely has some issues. I just decided early on that I needed to ask him. He's… he's so handsome and we know I can fall too hard too quickly, so I knew I needed to protect myself. I just plainly asked him and at first, he kind of shifted around the question and I felt like I was losing control of the conversation, but after a bit, he opened up. He seemed really vulnerable and honest."

"Ugh," she seems slightly annoyed. "How did you find such a good one? Where can I get one?"

"Maybe you should stop getting on dating apps and instead, try putting up dog walking flyers for yourself and making friends with an old, meddling woman who will try to set you up with a nice guy," I tease.

She laughs, "So, what you're really saying is, 'Thank you, Grace. You made this happen for me and I love you, and I don't know what I would do without you and you're the best friend in the entire world."

"Sure, that's what I'm saying," I joke but the reality is, she's not too far off. Things have changed quite a bit since she moved here and I'm starting to think it really might have been for the best.

TWELVE

Spring passes in a flurry between work, growing relationships and the blooming of love.

Richard has been home for a couple of months now and is recovering well. He occasionally walks Daisy with his physical therapist, and the at-home nurse they hired does a couple of walks a week with her as well. Louise does not like the at-home nurse. She finds her to be "nosey" and "annoying."

At this point, I don't think Louise even *needs* me to walk Daisy anymore. I think she just *likes* to talk to me and *wants* to keep me around… and I don't mind at all, because I like to talk to her too.

Austin has been slammed with work. He's been working probably fifty to sixty hours a week. The nice thing is, in the off-season, he normally only has to work twenty to thirty hours a week but I'm learning that spring is brutal for the landscaping industry.

Our relationship has been progressing slowly and steadily. Neither of us have done much dating before. I've been on a few dates over the years, but I've only had one "serious" boyfriend when I was in college. We dated for six months and it was all very surface level. Austin is basically in the same boat with only two past girlfriends and some sporadic dating. We're figuring it out together and I think that makes it special. We've taken time to get to know each other mentally and emotionally and are more than okay with waiting longer to move forward physically. It seems old-fashioned these days (and Grace keeps telling me I'm "crazy") but we want to wait until marriage. Although, we've only talked about it a handful of times because ultimately, it means we're mentioning marriage, and that scares us both a little.

It's mid-June, which means it's time for my dad's annual summer trip to visit. He's supposed to land any minute and normally, I can't wait for him to arrive, but this time, I'm nervous. He's going to meet Austin for the first-time tonight at dinner and it's been stressing me out. I've hardly been able to eat; I've been sleeping poorly, and I can't stop thinking about every possible scenario.

I don't know why I'm so anxious… or maybe, I do. I *want* my dad to like him. I *need* my dad to like him because I'm not sure what exactly I'll do if he doesn't…

Without my mom, my dad's opinion means everything to me. He was never the one I'd run to for advice about boys but now, he's all I have left. My mom's gone. My brother sucks. I've never been close to any extended family, and I only have a couple friends (and one of them is seventy-four). Obviously, Grace and Louise approve… making Dad the last piece of the puzzle.

(Dad) *Just landed! I didn't check a bag. I'll text when I'm outside.*

(Me) *Perfect! I am in the cell phone lot. See you soon!*

I haven't seen Dad since I went back home for the anniversary of Mom's passing, but we talk on a regular basis. He's heard about Austin, and he knows we've been dating for almost three months now. He knows I really like him and even though I haven't voiced it, I am sure he knows the importance of his meeting him. I've never played "meet the parents" before.

We're planning to go to dinner at J Peters in Carolina Forest. I'm hoping by going a little early and picking a place unknown to most tourists, we won't have a problem getting a table, despite it being peak summer.

(Dad) *I'm outside door three*

(Me) *Coming!*

I pull out of the cell phone lot and follow the winding road around to the terminal. I see Dad up ahead, standing at the curb with his suitcase. He waves when he sees my Ford Focus and I wave back.

"Dad!" I get out of the car and greet him with a hug.

"Emma Bear! I've missed you," he squeezes me lovingly.

"I've missed you too."

We load up his bags and he offers to drive back to my apartment.

"So, what do you want to do on your annual summer trip to Myrtle Beach?" I gesture out the window to the palm trees and blue skies.

"Well, for starters, I want to meet this man who's been seeing my baby girl."

"Dad!" I slap my palm to my forehead. "I know… but does that really have to be the first thing you bring up?"

"It's what I want to do most… so, yes!"

"I can still uninvite you, you know…" I mutter.

"But you won't."

He's right and he knows it.

"I guess I'd love to get in a round of golf and walk the beach a few mornings. Nothing crazy… you know I just like to come and spend time with you."

"I've told you; you should just move out here."

"I've tried," he argues.

"Daaad," I laugh. "You tried to buy a cabana you couldn't even sleep in. That's hardly trying at all."

"I know, I know," he joins in my laughter. "I'm sure I will someday… I don't know what I'm waiting for, but I can't quite let go."

I know what he means. For me, it was easy to leave, because I can always go back to visit him. But for him, if he sells the house, he's moving on. He can't go back. He'd leave a piece of mom there forever.

And so would I… so I don't *really* pressure him to leave. It will be okay when he does, and I'll love to have him closer but for now, I'll stick to visiting home and cherish the reminders of Mom scattered throughout it.

* * *

Dad, Grace, and I load up for dinner and head out just after five. I invited Grace for two reasons:

1. She's family, so duh.
2. I don't know anyone who can fill silence quite

like her and I want her there for backup. Dad is not a huge talker (that was always Mom) and Austin is relatively shy until you get to know him.

My desire for tonight to go well is starting to scare me. It must mean I really like him. It's only been three months, but it might actually be true what they say… "when you know, you know."

We've clicked on so many levels. We like the same music and television shows. We enjoy cooking meals and a good cup of coffee. We dream of the future and having two kids.

It's easy. It's simple. I'm starting to think I can fully trust him. But I can't say for certain. I hate trusting people. It's too exposing.

But… if tonight goes well. Maybe, I will fully let him in. If he gets along with my dad, maybe he deserves the whole story about my mom.

"Okay, Dad," I say as we get out of the car. "We've been over this a few times now but please, just because Austin is a landscaper does not mean you need to tell him your tree story."

"What tree story?" Dad acts confused.

"You *know* the tree story and it does *not* need to be told."

Austin is seated in a booth to the right when we walk into the restaurant, and he stands to greet us. I give him a hug but opt to forgo the kiss.

"Dad, this is Austin. Austin, this is my dad."

"It's nice to meet you Mr. Rivers," Austin reaches out his hand.

"You too," Dad gives it a firm shake. "You can call me Peter."

"How come I can't call you Peter?" Grace complains.

"I never said you couldn't," Dad replies.

"Oh, okay then… Peter," Grace sticks out her tongue like she tasted something bad. "Yeah, nah that's weird. I'll stick to Mr. Rivers."

I chuckle. "Okay, well now that we have that figured out," I gesture to the booth for us to sit down. I take a seat next to Austin and Dad sits directly across from me next to Grace.

"How was the flight?" Austin asks.

"It was good. No delays. Easy. All you can ask for," Dad answers.

"Well… not *all* you can ask for," Grace mutters. "I always tell you; you can use the plane."

"I don't need the plane," Dad waves his hand. "Commercial is just fine."

A young, brown-haired waiter approaches the table. "Good evening, y'all. What can I get you to drink?"

"I'll take a water please," I start.

"Me too," says Grace.

"Coke for me," Dad adds.

"I'll have the same," Austin answers.

"You got it," he finishes scribbling on his notepad and leaves the table.

"So, Emma tells me you're an accountant? How do you like it?"

"I love it. I really do… I know that sounds pretty lame, but I've always had a knack for numbers and it's enjoyable to me."

"That's great. And you have your own firm now, right?"

"Yeah, I mostly do consulting work now and I have two employees. It's nothing much but I like it more than corporate America. After twenty-five years in it, I was ready to step out."

"And how long have you been out of it again?"

"Oh gosh, probably ten years or so now. I wanted more flexibility when the kids were in high school."

"I'm sure it was nice to get to be around more when they were growing up."

I don't know what I was worried about. Austin is even more charming than I imagined he could be with Dad.

"Yeah, I loved it. I'll always cherish those years as a family…" Dad trails off. He snaps back, "but that's enough about me. Tell me about you. I hear you work in landscaping?"

"I do. My grandpa started the business about forty-five years ago and I took it over after I graduated from college."

"Wow. That's great. It's not an easy industry… especially in this Myrtle Beach heat."

"That's true. Fortunately, I mostly manage now and do behind the scenes stuff, but I've worked my fair share of yards in the sun, and it can be brutal."

"You know, I'm no stranger to yard work myself," Dad starts and thankfully the waiter comes back and interrupts.

"Here are those drinks for you," he sets them on the table. "Are you guys ready to order or do you need another minute?"

We all take turns looking at one another saying, "I can be ready if you go first," and "Uhh I can be."

Grace speaks up for us all. "I think another minute or two would be great."

"You got it."

"What were you saying?" Austin politely asks once the waiter is gone.

"You don't need to know," I answer. "He promised me he wouldn't tell the story." I accusingly glare at Dad. "Anyway, he loves a good toast. Dad… take it away."

"I do love a good toast." He picks up his glass and

we all join him. "To good dinners, great company and good tree stories."

Ugh, I guess I set him up for that one. We clink our glasses and take sips.

"Ahh so it's about a tree? I want to hear it. I'm sure it's a good one," Austin prompts.

"I assure you, it's not."

"Yeah, it's not," Grace agrees.

Dad tells it anyway. "One time, a few years back, when Emma was a sophomore in high school, we had a big tree out back… probably thirty or forty feet high–"

"Probably twenty," I correct. "It gets taller every time you tell it."

"Whatever height," Dad continues, unfazed, "And it was dead, so I decided to take it down branch by branch. Each week, when it was trash day, I'd take down a few limbs, break them up and fit whatever I could in the garbage can. It took me a good year and a half, but I saved us quite a bit of money and I took out that whole tree by myself."

"Wow, that's very impressive," Austin sounds genuine.

Does he actually think it's impressive? It's such a lame story.

"We don't do much with trees, but I know they can be very expensive to take out."

"Yes, I think someone quoted me nearly $1,500 to do it and I said, 'no, I can do it myself' and I sure did."

I place my hand to my forehead. Why did I even bother trying to tell him not to tell it? I'm probably the one who gave him the idea… although, he does tell it every chance he gets anyway. He's so embarrassing.

"That's awesome!"

"It's less 'awesome' if you heard him talk about it every week for the year and a half it took him to take it down and then retell the story every chance he gets," Grace laughs.

"I remember how excited Mom, you, and I were when he finally had one week left. We thought we'd finally stop hearing about the stupid tree, and we couldn't wait… but lo and behold, here we are nine years later, and still hearing about it," I shake my head and we all laugh.

I guess I'll ask Austin later what he really thinks, but for now, I am glad we're all chatting easily and sharing stories… even if they aren't the ones I wanted.

* * *

All in all, dinner went well, and I think everyone had a good time, although I haven't been able to talk to Dad or Austin alone much. After dinner, everyone came back to our apartment and played games. Then, on Saturday, Dad and Austin golfed together, went to lunch and looked for shells on the beach before coming back to the apartment to hang out again.

It took about half of the weekend, seeing them bonding, for me to finally put two and two together. Austin never really had a father and Dad's son disowned him. They're sort of a match made in heaven.

It's Sunday morning and finally, I am going to get some time alone with Dad to see what he thinks. I assume he likes him… considering he's ditched me all weekend to hang out with him… but I am still anxious to talk.

"You ready?" I find Dad in the kitchen after I've finished getting ready in Grace's bathroom. I used to sleep on an air mattress in the second bedroom when he came to visit and give him my bedroom, but now that Grace occupies the second bedroom, I slept on the couch. Her bathroom doubles as the guest bath when people come over, so it makes it easy to get ready in there and give Dad my whole suite.

"You bet," he smiles up from his book.

"I'm excited for you to meet Louise," I say as we head out the door. "She's quite the woman. Full of spunk and personality. She actually reminds me a lot of Mom."

"I'm excited to meet her. You've been walking her dog for a while now, right?"

"Yeah, like three and a half months or so… I started walking Daisy a couple weeks before I met Austin."

"Right, because she 'set you guys up,'" Dad makes quotation marks with his hands.

"Right," I confirm. We get in the car and buckle our seatbelts in near perfect unison, shifting the seatbelt from our outside to inside hand halfway. It's odd the little things you pick up from other people in life. The totally miniscule and meaningless things you mindlessly mimic like those around you. "She still won't admit it was a setup though," I laugh.

"Maybe it wasn't," Dad shrugs.

"Dad," I roll my eyes. "She told me Sunday she wanted to set me up and I politely declined… then, Thursday morning, I show up to walk Daisy at the same time I always do and it 'just so happens' she scheduled Austin to come by for a landscaping quote… no, I don't think so," I laugh. "Sounds a little too premeditated for my liking."

"Premeditated?" Dad chuckles. "She tried to set you up with a guy… not murder you."

"Okay, fine. 'Premediated' sounds a bit harsh… but planned at least."

"I can probably agree with that… she really does

sound like mom: always meddling in other people's lives."

"True," we both laugh.

"At least she set you up with such a nice guy though."

"Yeah? You really think so? You like him?"

"I do. They say you're not supposed to like your daughter's boyfriend... that no one will be good enough for your little girl... but the truth is, Emma Bear, I haven't found anything to dislike about the guy."

"Ahh, I'm so glad," relief washes over my body. "I was nervous for you guys to meet and then I haven't gotten to talk to either one of you... because you've been so busy hanging out with one another... so I assumed it was going well but I am SO glad! I think I really like him, Dad."

"He really seems like a good one."

We sit in silence for a few moments before I finally ask the question eating up at my mind.

"Do you think Mom would approve?"

Without hesitation and with the utmost sincerity, Dad assures me, "I think she'd love him."

* * *

"Good morning." Louise is sitting outside when we walk

through the gate. "This is my dad." I gesture toward him. "I convinced him to come walk Daisy with me this morning."

"Morning," her voice sounds extra raspy today. She stands from her rocker and shakes Dad's hand. "It's a pleasure to meet you."

"You as well. Emma has said the nicest things about you."

"Oh, I have nothing but the best things to say about Emma. I truly think she's an angel."

That's the nicest compliment I've ever received.

"She's a good one," he agrees.

"No, I really mean it. I don't know how I could have gotten by these last few months without her. She really saved my life."

No, *that's* the nicest compliment ever.

"It's not been a big deal." I wave my hand nonchalantly, though my heart is warm with affection. "I've been happy to do it."

Well, mostly… I can't believe I tried to get out of walking Daisy. What if I never showed up? Never met Louise? Or Austin? Life is truly both terrifying and remarkable when you piece together all of the small decisions and see how they've become the roadmap of your life.

"Where is Daisy?" I realize she's not outside.

"Oh, she's being a prima donna this morning… she didn't want to come out."

"Do you want me to get her?"

"If you don't mind."

I walk to the back door and call for Daisy after opening it. She howls and comes running excitedly toward me.

"She loves Emma," I hear Louise comment to Dad as I hook up Daisy's leash. "I love Emma too," she continues. "We were never able to have children and she's kind of become like a granddaughter to me."

Gosh, now maybe *that's* the nicest compliment.

"Well, from the sounds of it, Emma feels the same about you. She never really got to know her grandparents… my parents died before she was born, and Eleanor's parents didn't come around too much. I'm sure she cherishes your relationship."

"I do," I lovingly pat Louise on the back. This is getting a little too mushy-gushy, lovey-dovey for me this morning. "Should we get to walking?"

"Let's do it," Dad agrees.

"I'll be here when you get back. It's a beautiful day out. Enjoy!"

When we're out the back gate and walking down the driveway, Dad comments, "She's very nice. I can see why you two get along."

"What do you mean?" his wording catches me off guard.

"You can tell she's been a bit hardened by the world. She hasn't had it easy and that bothers her, but it doesn't stop her."

I don't know what to say. His words feel slightly harsh but also complimentary.

"You think I'm 'hardened?'"

"I think you've had some very difficult experiences that make it hard to open up and trust others. I think she has too… and I think that's a big reason you get along… Despite not generally trusting people, you've decided you can trust each other."

"You got all of that out of that small encounter?" I skeptically raise my eyebrow.

"I feel like I can read people pretty well," he shrugs.

He's right. I hadn't thought about it that way before. Since Mom died, I hadn't let anyone new in until Louise. Sure, I made a few friends here and there but nothing more than cordial acquaintanceships. And after no time at all with her, I was telling her about my mother and brother, and she was setting me up on a date.

"Well… two negatives *do* make a positive," I laugh.

"That's true," Dad chuckles. "I'm glad you found her…" he hesitates, and I already know what he's going to say. "It's nice for you to have a motherly influence in your life again."

Despite ignoring every inkling, feeling and emotion

I've had toward Louise, I knew that was true all along…
I just hadn't dared to admit it. She feels like home.

THIRTEEN

I Can't Tonight

Summer turns to fall to winter to spring in the usual way and my relationship with Austin progresses. We agree on all the big things (faith, family, lifestyle) and disagree on all the little things (chocolate versus vanilla, which way the toilet paper should hang, and how to load the dishwasher), the way the best couples do. It doesn't take long for me to know he's my person. I want to spend the rest of my life with him.

* * *

"I think he's going to propose," I tell Louise as we sit in her living room. Daisy is laying at my feet, seemingly extra tired from today's walk.

"Do you really?" she smiles. "What makes you think that?"

"I just have a feeling. I can't really pinpoint it. The only 'clue,'" I make quotation marks with my hands, "I have is I think he asked my dad when we were home for Easter last weekend. "I don't know when, I just think he did… That and the fact that he's been acting super weird."

"Weird?" she raises an eyebrow.

"Yeah, the guy can hardly hold a conversation with me. Either he's trying to break up with me and can't get up the nerve, or he's planning something."

"You're probably right," she smiles a warm and genuine smile. "Can you believe it was only a little over a year ago when I first called you? I was so desperate for help for Daisy, and I found an angel."

It's not the first, or even second time, she's called me an angel, but it still catches me off guard. I can't think of a nicer compliment and, more than that, I swear she believes it. I genuinely think she thinks I'm her angel. But I really don't know who's helping whom in this relationship because I swear, she's *my* guardian angel.

"It's so wild," I agree. "And really, it's all thanks to you."

"I know you didn't trust my match making skills in the beginning… had to create a casual run-in to get the whole thing started –"

"I knew it!" I interrupt. "Finally," I toss my head back and a smile washes over my face, "You admit it!"

"Of course," Louise grins. "You knew the whole time… Did I really have to tell you?"

"Well, you didn't *have* to, but you also didn't *have* to change the subject every time I asked either," I laugh.

"Touché," she agrees. "So, when do you think he'll ask?"

"I don't know," I sigh. "We've talked about it a couple of times before and I told him I want something very sweet and intimate. I don't want it to be a whole thing with lots of people and what not… I just want it to be the two of us. Which is great for what I want, but not great for guessing when it will happen… considering it could quite literally be anytime."

"True," Louise agrees.

"How did Richard propose to you?" I realize I've never heard the story.

"Oh, it was nothing much. We went out to dinner one evening at a restaurant near the boardwalk, that's no longer there, and after the meal, he got down on one knee and asked me to marry him."

"That's nice."

"Yeah, it was nothing fancy, but it was us. We've never been anything fancy. Just a simple love. The best kind."

I think about that and meditate on its truth. My parent's love was nothing like the movies… but in the best way. It was kind, tender, and compassionate. It wasn't filled with the insane highs and lows: the passionate exuberance and countering feverish vexation. It was simple. Real. Perfect.

As more time inserts itself between when I last saw my mother and father together, I know the glasses get rosier. But what do I have left of her and their relationship if not a rosy retrospective?

"Yeah, my parents had that kind of love." *Had.* Ugh. Grammar is relentless.

"Did they? You never talk much about your mother."

"They did. It was nothing fancy; just pure, unconditional love. Dad has never really recovered from her death." Can I blame him though? It's not like I have either. "It's hard to talk about her."

"Hey, would you look at me?"

I hadn't realized I'd stopped making eye contact with her. I look up and meet her dark green eyes.

"I know I never knew her, and I didn't know your relationship, but she would be so proud of who you've become. I have to imagine you've surpassed her wildest dreams about who you would become. I don't meet many kids like you these days. You are truly special, Emma."

My eyes instinctively begin to water. "Thank you." I try to blink the tears away, but a few slip out. "Do you think she'd like Austin? Do you think she'd want me to marry him?"

"Oh, honey. I know she would. I've known Austin his entire life and I've never met a soul who didn't like him. I promise you; she would not be the exception."

"Thank you." The thought warms my heart. "I think you would have liked her. I could see you guys getting along."

"I would have loved to meet her."

In an effort to not cry again, I try to shift back to lighthearted fun. "You guys would have been great at sharing pizza too," I chuckle. "Only two people I've ever met who need spicy honey drizzled over it."

"Mmm, cheese pizza with a bit of hot honey…" she licks her lips at the thought. "Nothing better."

"I have to know… what made you want to try that? It's so random and I never got to ask my mom."

"I don't know," she shrugs. "I only discovered it within the last ten years or so… one day it just sounded delicious, and I had both, so I gave it a whirl… never went back."

"She could never convince me to try it," I turn my nose up.

"You can't hate it until you try it," Louise chides.

"I'll tell you like I used to tell her, 'Watch me.'" I wink.

She shakes her head and we both laugh.

* * *

Austin is back to the grind of busy season and my vacation days are about to expire if I don't use them, which leads to a perfect storm on this Friday. I decide I am going to surprise him with dinner at the end of his workday. Things have been crazy lately, he's seemed a bit off, and I want some good, quality time with him.

I pick up a couple of sandwiches for us on the way to the beach house he's been working at nonstop this month. It's one of his biggest projects to date and I can tell the stress is getting to him. I park at the end of the driveway and see Austin talking to a few workers on the front porch. He does a double take when he notices my car, and though he waves, he doesn't look very excited to see me.

It's the end of what is probably a busy day at the end of a busy week, so I assume he's just tired. Unbothered, I wave back, and get out of the car.

"Surprise! I brought us some dinner," I hold up the bag of food as I walk up the porch steps.

"Hey, I… I really appreciate it… but I was planning to get some dinner with the guys tonight."

"Oh, I'm sorry," I apologize but I'm not totally sure why, I have nothing to be sorry about. I was trying to do a nice thing. "I didn't realize you had plans."

"Yeah, I thought I told you Cole was coming to visit this weekend. He's staying with Landon, but we planned to all go out tonight."

Of course, Austin has friends… and I've met several of them… but he's never been much of a "hang with the bros" kind of guy. I'm completely caught off guard.

"Oh… well, okay then." I feel my phone vibrating in my pocket, and I am thankful for a distraction because I'm at a loss for words. I pull it out and see Grace is calling. "One sec," I tell Austin before answering. "Hey."

"Hey, what are you doing tonight?"

"I *guess* nothing," I emphasize the reply for Austin to hear.

"Well, I just scored tickets to Copper Sticks in Charleston tonight. If we leave now, we can make it there and be back by like midnight. They're opening for some other band, and I already scoped them out… the main act sounds like garbage, so we don't have to stay."

"You want to drive four hours round trip tonight for Copper Sticks?" I like the band okay, but I don't have the same desire.

"Come ooon," she begs. "What else are you doing?"

And suddenly, I'm reminded of what I'm *not* doing tonight. If Austin can "hang with the bros," then I can go to Charleston with my bestie.

"Okay, sure! I'm up for the adventure!"

"Yaaayyy!" She sings. "Where are you now and what are you wearing?"

"I'm near Forty-Fourth Avenue and," I look down to remind myself but hesitate because I know she won't approve.

She cuts in again before I can answer. "You know what, it's only 4:45 p.m. We don't need to leave here until 5:15 p.m. Can you come home right now? I'll pick something out for you, and you can do your makeup on the way."

"Okay," I'm not thrilled about her plans, but they do sound better than sitting at home and thinking about Austin ditching me all night. "Be home in ten."

* * *

Less than thirty minutes later, we're driving south down seventeen. Grace laid out a rust orange, corduroy romper. I haven't worn it before, and I am pleasantly surprised at the fit. Its tank top straps lay comfortably on my shoulders, and the faux-wrap belt flatters my waist. She paired it with short, black leather booties and small gold hoop earrings. Normally, when she lends me her clothes, I never care to wear them again, but I like this one. I might actually have to stow it away in my closet. She'll never notice (and even if she did, she wouldn't care).

"Here." Grace hands me a very light, almost nude pink nail polish she pulls out of her purse. "I brought you this too."

"Why?" I shoot her a disapproving look.

"Because your nails are not looking their best."

"Rude," I scoff. "Who cares if they look good at a dimly lit concert venue?"

"You should care," Grace quickly retorts.

I roll my eyes and sigh, signaling both my resistance and surrender.

Grace turns up the music and I do my makeup. We exchange a few words here and there but for the most part, it's quiet. I think we're both happy to have made it to the weekend. It's not until I finish painting my nails that I decide I want to talk about what's on my mind.

"Austin totally ditched me," I say out of nowhere. I hold my hands up in front of the air vents to help them dry.

"What?" Grace is shocked. "When? Why?"

"Tonight. I went to surprise him with food at the end of his workday, that's where I was when you called about the concert, and he told me he was going to 'hang

with the bros,'" I use my best low, obnoxious imperson-
ation of a man's voice.

"Really? That's so unlike him."

"I know! He's been acting crazy lately. At first, I
thought it was because he was going to propose… I was
convinced he was just acting weird because he was nervous but now, I swear he wants to break up with me and
he's too scared to actually do it."

"No… Emma. You can't really think that. Surely
not?"

"I don't know, Grace," I throw up my hands. "He's
been *so* strange. I feel like I can't even talk to him lately.
I ask him how work is going and it's like he's never heard
the question before. He can hardly answer. He stumbles
over all his words. It's like his brain isn't working."

"He's really busy this time of year… maybe he's just
been distracted."

"*And* in over a year of dating, he's never once left
me to hang out with the guys… in fact, a few times, I've
had to convince him he should hang out with them instead of me… and now, he just ditches me when I try to
be nice and surprise him? I mean really… what even is
that?!"

"I'm sorry, Emma. He's head over heels for you
though… we both know that. He probably just has a lot
going on."

"I don't know… I guess." In my head, I know she's right. He does love me, and things are going well. We're great together. Surely, it's just a blip…. an odd season of life.

"He loves you, Emma! I'm sure it's nothing…" She playfully shoves me. "And you're with me tonight anyways. Just like old times… we're going to have a blast!"

"Okay, okay," I relent. "You're right. We're going to have fun!"

We listen to Copper Sticks the rest of the drive and it does, indeed, feel like old times. It feels like we could be in high school again, driving on any Texas backroad, with our windows down and nowhere to go. It's not until we cross the Cooper River Bridge that I even think to ask what venue we're going to.

"I think it's called Charleston Pour House," Grace answers.

"You think? Where are your directions going to?"

Her phone is plugged into the car, and I pick it up to open her maps.

"It's taking us to the Pineapple Fountain. I coordinated with the ticket guy to meet him there."

"Wait? You don't have the tickets? Where did you find this guy?"

"Craigslist."

"What? I didn't even know you knew Craigslist existed. So, we just drove two hours to meetup with a random guy for these tickets. What if he doesn't show?"

Grace shrugs. "What if he does?"

"How are you so optimistic all of the time?"

"I don't know... how are you so pessimistic?"

I roll my eyes and don't voice a reply.

"It's not a big deal. If we get there and he doesn't show, oh well. We'll grab dinner in the city and walk around. *And* if we get there and he *does* show, we'll have a head banging time at the concert." Before I can reply, she cranks the music up earsplittingly loud and starts whipping her head back and forth.

A few minutes later, we find a parking spot on the street, and she leads us to the fountain... or better yet, tries to lead us. There's a lot of construction and it feels like we're going in circles.

"Where are we going? I swear we've already passed that building three times."

She looks at her phone. "I don't know. I'm so confused... it says to turn here but it's like hidden in this park or something maybe."

We walk through a residential-feeling section with townhouses lining the sidewalks. Eventually, the buildings end and we can see the water up ahead.

"This feels promising."

"Yes, I think if we take a right when we get to the park, it should be pretty close," Grace replies.

We make it to the park and turn right down a herringbone brick sidewalk. It's lined with trees and benches and the sun is starting to set, speckling the sky with oranges and pinks. It's the kind of picturesque landscape you can't quite capture in a photograph.

"Do you think that could be him?" Grace points ahead to a man in a hoodie facing the opposite direction.

"Maybe?"

We're steps away from the fountain when the man turns around and immediately, I stop in my tracks.

"Austin?" My brain is hardly working. It feels like I took a sip of something I wasn't expecting. Like I ordered a coke, but they gave me sweet tea and it's still delicious but out of place.

Without saying a word, he takes off his hoodie, unveiling a cream button down shirt, and reaches out his hand. I take hold of it and my heart races with anticipation. He walks me around the fountain to the side closest to the water. Only now do I see a white blanket decorated with vases of white flowers and pillar candles. He leads me to the center of it and grabs my other hand. He looks into my eyes, and I can hardly breath.

"Emma, I love you so much, and I couldn't imagine spending the rest of my life with anyone else. You're my best friend and you make me a better person each and every day. I love making you happy and I would love it if you gave me the honor of making you happy for the rest of our lives…" He gets down on one knee and opens a black, velvet box. "Emma Katherine Rivers, will you marry me?"

"Yes," I breath out the word. "Yes!"

He slips the ring onto my finger, and I lean down to kiss him. I put my hands on the sides of his face and soak it all in. A few passersby clap and shout their congratulations.

He stands and engulfs me in a hug. It's only when he lets go that I think to actually look at the ring. When I see it, I'm stunned. It flaunts a gorgeous diamond with a simple, white gold band.

"Do you like it?" he sees me looking at the ring.

I know nothing about the quality of diamonds or gold, and I do not care. It's beautiful. It's perfect. It's mine.

"I love it," I smile up at him. "I love you!" I kiss him again. It feels impossible to express all my adoration in this moment.

"I'm sorry you thought I was ditching you. I hated doing that… you're just so hard to surprise and I wanted it to be perfect."

"It… it was incredible… *is* incredible. How did you do all of this?"

"I had lots of help," he gestures around, and I suddenly remember we're not alone.

"Ahh!" I run to Grace and throw my arms around her.

"Congratulations! I'm so happy for you both!" She squeezes me tight.

I let go and put my hands on my cheeks. They're warm with excitement and surprise.

I hear the click of a camera behind me and turn to see a face I haven't met before holding it.

"Emma, this is Cole. Cole, this is Emma." Austin introduces us.

I shake his hand. "It's nice to meet you."

"You too."

"Cole is a photographer. He normally shoots sports, but I thought he'd capture the moment well," Austin pats his back.

"I think I got some great shots."

"I'm sure you did," Grace slides into the conversation. "Grace," she holds out her hand.

"Cole," he shakes it and smiles.

The original plan for the evening crosses my mind. "Wait," I grab ahold of Austin's arm with both my hands, "Are we still going to the concert?"

"Oh, um…" He looks concerned and starts to ramble. "No, I uh… this was the whole plan… I'm so sorry.

I didn't even think about that aspect… I'm sure we could buy tickets at the door…"

"Austin," I squeeze his arm. "I'm relieved. Don't worry. I was only going for Grace and… well because you ditched me," I laugh. "This is perfect. It's all perfect."

He kisses me and I kiss him back. I've never in my life been happier.

* * *

We stay a while and walk in the park, enjoying the water view and high of the night.

Cole and Grace clean up everything and head back to Myrtle together. I can only imagine their car ride. It was clear to me that Grace was interested in him… poor Cole. She's relentless when she wants something. Though he did seem like her type… and I wouldn't mind double dating… so I guess I'll cross my fingers.

"Would you want to get dinner? I was thinking we could stop in Georgetown on the way back." Austin leads the way to his car.

"That's great with me." I look down at my hand and admire my ring for the one-thousandth time tonight.

The entire evening has been a magical blur and it's not even over.

"So," Austin looks to me with a wide grin as he starts the car. "When are we going to get married?"

My mind is spinning with plans and announcements and invitations and emotions, and I don't quite know where to start. It's like a long line of dominoes in my brain and I can't find the beginning. I know once I do, they will all start falling, but first, I need to sort them out.

"Oh my goodness. I don't even know," I beam. "I've always wanted a fall wedding. Maybe next year?"

"Fall would be nice. What about this year?"

"This year?! What? Are you crazy?" I jokingly raise my voice. "Even if we did October, that would only be six months to plan the wedding."

"So?"

"*So*, you need more than six months to plan a wedding."

"Nah, we can do it."

Fall of this year? Six months from now?

Crazy.

Although… it does sound nice.

I could probably plan a wedding in six months. I mean, how hard could it really be? We both have small families and not a lot of friends.

Heck, I could probably plan it in six weeks.

"What?" I laugh. "Where is this coming from?"

"I don't know," he shrugs. "I'm just elated. I would marry you this instant! I can't believe you said, 'yes!'"

"You really thought I would say, 'no?'"

"I don't know. No… I'm just happy. I can hardly think."

"Same," I agree but it's not true. I never stop thinking. "It's a lot to take in."

"Agreed… but you know what I *do* know?"

We're stopped at a light, and he looks over at me. His eyes warm and genuine.

"What's that?"

"That I love you and I can't wait to spend the rest of my life with you."

I kiss him. "I love you too."

FOURTEEN

The Wedding Bells Are Ringing

Wedding planning is in full swing when Dad comes to visit. It didn't take long for Austin to convince me six months was plenty of time to plan the wedding… just thinking about getting to call him mine forever sooner did the trick.

"Whoa," Dad comments when he walks in the apartment. He'd been out golfing, and, in the meantime, Grace and I covered the entire kitchen table (not that it's that big, but still) with color palettes, pictures, mock invitations, fabric samples and more.

"This feels pretty far out of my league but…" he hesitates to offer, "What can I help with?"

"Just keep your checkbook handy," Grace teases.

"Oh, I've already had that out a time or two" Dad laughs.

"You're good for now," I smile. "Austin will be coming over in a little while and then we have the tasting this afternoon. Why don't you get cleaned up and the two of you can keep each other entertained, while Grace and I try to make some decisions over here. With three and a half months to go, it's getting to be crunch time."

I think Dad senses my stress because he comes to give me a hug. "It will all work out. Don't stress… it will be a perfect day."

"Thanks, Dad," I hug him back. "And I'm serious about that shower," I wrinkle my nose at his sweaty stench.

"Okay, okay," he laughs. "I get it. I will shower and stay out of the way."

* * *

A little while later, Austin arrives and the four of us head to DeeDee's Catering. It's a local catering shop in downtown Conway and everyone we've talked to raves about it.

"For the entrees, I ordered chicken parmesan, roasted pork loin, chicken marsala, and cavatappi with vodka sauce for us to try. We'll need to pick two. Then, she said they'd pick a few vegetable and potato sides for us to taste, as well as their house salad and dinner rolls.

I'm not exactly sure what, if anything, we need to pick of those, but I am sure she will tell us."

"Sounds delicious!" Austin smacks his lips. "Thanks for getting this all set up." He reaches his hand to the back seat without taking his eyes off the road and I grab it. He gives me a loving squeeze. He knows I'm a bit worried with the quick timeline, so he compensates with overwhelming encouragement.

"Yes, it does!" Dad agrees. "But what I want to know is when we get to try the wedding cake."

Dad has always had an immense sweet tooth. The richer the better in his book.

"We already have the cake taken care of," Grace answers. "No taste test needed."

"What?" Dad drops his draw. "No taste test? What kind of wedding planning is this? The cake is the best part!"

"Part of my parent's gift to Emma and Austin is the cake," Grace answers. "Mom hired our favorite pastry chef from Dallas to make the cake and they're going to fly it out here."

"Oh, they're going to fly it out here now, are they?" Dad mocks a British accent in an attempt to sound high class. "I wouldn't dare have it any other way."

Grace sticks out her tongue and rolls her eyes.

"It's very nice of the Joneses to offer to do that," I

defend. "Chef Durand's pastries are some of the best I've ever had. I'm sure the cake will be delicious."

"I know, I know. I'm only teasing," Dad laughs. "You know I have to give Grace a hard time every now and again. Otherwise, who will?"

He's right. Grace is an only child with parents who do anything and everything for her, and even though she's two months younger than me, I've never picked on her like a little sister. She makes the rules and I'm her subordinate. For the health of everyone, someone has to give her a hard time, and over the years, that person has always been Dad.

"Ahh, yes, darling," Grace retorts in her own mock British accent, "If no one would push against me, I'd simply explode."

Everyone laughs and my heart warms with gratitude for these people around me. Life is good.

* * *

"I vote chicken marsala and chicken parmesan," Dad starts the opinion giving after we've all tasted the plethora of options spread across our table.

"You can't have two chicken options," Grace replies. "I say the pork loin and the chicken marsala."

"I didn't really like the pork loin, but then again, I don't really care for meat other than chicken," I shrug.

"Okay, well if we want one chicken option and one not chicken option, we need to pick the between the marsala and parmesan and then between the pork loin and cavatappi," Austin reasons.

"True," I appreciate his direction. "So, pork loin or cavatappi."

"Pork loin."

"Cavatappi."

"Pork loin."

The votes come in before I can even process and suddenly, I'm left with the deciding vote. "Well, if I pick pork loin, it's a clear winner and cavatappi makes it a tie, which makes it complicated and I don't like complicated, so pork loin it is."

"Fair," Dad agrees with my reasoning, though he was outvoted.

"And now parmesan or marsala? And I vote marsala because I don't want to be stuck with last vote this time."

"Marsala."

"Marsala."

"It's unanimous," Austin nods. "I vote marsala as well."

"Yum! It was all delicious." Dad wipes his mouth with a napkin.

"It really was. I'm happy to have another thing checked off the list."

"Hello," Austin answers a phone call I didn't hear

ring. He listens intently. "Oh, no," he wrinkles his forehead. I can't hear the person well on the other end, but it sounds like a woman. The rest of the call follows with only one side of the information.

"When?"

"Where is she now?"

"Okay, we will head that way."

My stomach has a sinking feeling.

"That was my grandma," Austin says after hanging up the phone. "Louise is in the hospital. It sounds like they think she had a stroke, but she didn't know for sure. The ambulance left her house about an hour ago."

"Are they taking her to Grand Strand or Tidelands?" I'm thankful Grace has words to say because I can't really think of any.

I can't lose Louise. I just can't. Not now.

"Grand Strand."

"Do we need to do anything else here?" Dad asks. "Or can we go?"

"We can go. The tasting was complimentary, and I'm supposed to email her with our selections by the end of the month. We just need to leave a tip for our server."

Dad pulls out his wallet and sets a twenty-dollar bill on the table.

We clear out in a rush and drive the thirty minutes to the hospital without many words exchanged.

This can't be happening. Maybe it was a mistake, and it wasn't a big deal. Old people have issues all the time that turn out to be nothing. I'm sure it's nothing.

"We're here for Louise Walters," Austin informs the nurse at the rounded desk.

"Hey," Richard calls from across the lobby. I've only seen Richard a few times. He's not normally around when I walk Daisy or chat with Louise, but I recognize him right away.

He's sitting in a wooden chair, his shoulders hunched over. His hair is a thin, light gray and his rounded glasses elongate his face. He's wearing a gray sweater with a plaid collared shirt sticking out of the top and khaki slacks. Either he was getting ready to go out, or Louise made him change before heading to the hospital (either option seems probable). She always complains about people out and about looking like they just woke up and rolled out of bed. She would never be caught dead out of the house with sweatpants and no makeup. I shudder. Not my best idiom at the moment.

"Oh, we're with him," Austin half tells the nurse as we all make our way to sit by Richard. "Hey," he takes the seat to his right. "How is she? How are you?"

"Doing okay," he weakly answers. "We were watching television in the den, and she said she was going to grab a snack from the kitchen. Next thing I knew, she was on the ground, unconscious."

"That's really scary." Austin pats Richard's back a few times before leaving his hand there.

"It is… the paramedics at the house said they think it could have been a mini stroke, that it might not have even been a full blown one." Richard's leg starts nervously shaking. "But still, especially given her heart history, it's scary."

I cross my legs and rest my chin in my hands. I often see my thoughts in color, but right now, they're black and white. My whole mind feels dark and silent.

I don't know how much time has passed when Dad walks up and sits next to me. I hadn't even noticed he'd left in the first place.

"How are you doing?" he puts his arm around me.

"Okay, I guess," I shrug. "It's hard when we don't know anything."

"Yeah," he rubs my back. "It sounds like Richard is concerned but not overly worried."

Have we been listening to the same person? He seems terrified to me.

"I'm sure everything is going to be okay."

Suddenly, the parallel is too real and my mind is no longer black and white. It's red with blood and the crimson stain of the night my mother died.

* * *

Bodies buzz around me as music blares and everything slowly becomes a steady blur. The alcohol runs through my veins, taking me to a place of tranquility. A place I've never experienced before.

"How are you feeling?" I hear Grace shout at me over the thudding bass.

"Great!" I shout back and bob out of rhythm to the music. I swing my red solo cup slightly above my head as liquid sloshes out of it with every movement.

"Are you sure you're okay?" Grace raises her eyebrows. "Em, I've never seen you like this." She tries to grab the cup out of my hand, and I yank it back.

"I told you. I'm greaaaat!"

"You need to cool it with this," she rips the cup out of my hand. "You've never had liquor before, and you've already had too much. Let's get out of here." She tosses the cup on the ground, spilling sticky liquid everywhere, and grabs my arm.

"No," I resist her grip. "Not until I kiss Dylan."

"Emma. You don't want to kiss that guy."

"Oh, yes, I do… I want to do more than that with him."

"No, you don't. The guy's a jerk and this party blows. Let's go home."

No, it doesn't. It's the coolest party I've ever been to… and only… but who cares? Still the coolest and I'm not leaving until I'm good and ready.

"No, I don't want to go home! I'm *not* going home."

"Okay, you don't have to go *home*. You can go back to my house. I don't like seeing you like this, Em. I thought I wanted rebel Emma, but I don't. I like simple, rule-following, kind Emma. Not this."

"*Ugh!* I'm so sick of that Emma. She's the worst," I roll my eyes as far into my head as they'll go. "Emma who never has any fun. Emma who goes to stupid concerts just to make her mom happy. Emma who pleases everyone. Blah, blah, blah. She's such a bore."

"She's not a bore. Emma, please. Let's go." She grabs my arm again.

"No!" My body feels like a wet noodle, but I manage to rip it away and run to the center of the living room where Dylan is talking in a circle with a few other guys.

"Emma!" I faintly hear Grace calling my name as she follows me through the crowd. "Emma!"

I reach up, grab the sides of Dylan's face, and pull his lips to mine. An electric pulse runs through my body, and I feel his tongue in my mouth. I feel hands on my shoulders, and I think their Dylan's, until I realize his hands are moving down my back. Before he reaches my butt, the other hands pull me from him.

"Get your grimy hands off of her, you asshole!" Grace yells and slaps him once across the face.

"Grace! What are you doing?" I'm utterly mortified. The living room is quiet. All eyes have shifted to watch the action.

"This sleazebag has been hitting on me all night and he tried to kiss me earlier."

The room spins harder than it already was, and I feel sick.

"I'm sorry, Emma. I wanted to leave. Let's get out of here."

I suppress every urge I have to throw up. I'm already dreading going back to school on Monday and if I throw up, I might have to finish the year home schooling.

Grace puts her arm around me, and I lean heavily on her. The alcohol suddenly feels like lead in my veins.

I open my eyes and find myself leaning my head against the window of her car. I don't remember getting there, but I am thankful for the cool glass against my warm skin. I don't say anything. I don't have anything to say. I don't feel like myself at all. I have no idea what's gotten into me.

"I'm sorry, Emma. I should have told you before you got to him. I wanted to protect you."

"It's not your fault," is all I can muster. It's never your fault. Nothing ever is. Everything works out for you. Everyone loves you. Must be nice.

We ride in silence for a while longer… my mind spinning with the worst of thoughts… I think I can keep them down… like I always do… but then, the liquid courage overtakes me.

"Why do you even bother hanging out with me? You could do so much better."

"I really couldn't, Em. You're the realist, most loyal friend a girl could ask for. Those idiots back there," she points and even in my current state of mind, I know it's the wrong direction. She's never been good at geography. "They have nothing on you. I couldn't care less about them."

"I'm not sure about that. I think you only hang out with me because I'm a pity project to you. I'm the dainty, helpless nerd you can transform like it's some kind of lame, nineties movie."

Grace's face flashes with angst. I hurt her feelings. I guess I'm trying to ruin all my relationships in one night.

Her phone starts ringing and "Mr. Rivers" flashes up on the screen.

"Oh, no." My stomach sinks.

Grace reaches for the screen, and I hit her hand away.

"Are you crazy? Don't answer it. Oh my gosh. I'm dead. I'm so dead."

"I was going to decline it."

"Well, don't do that either. That seems more suspicious." Both the alcohol and adrenaline are starting to wear off and anxiety is beginning to overtake me.

The call finally stops ringing and I take a deep breath. At least we bought some time.

"Why don't you take me back to my house? Maybe I can sneak in the window again and pretend it was a misunderstanding… that I was sick in the bathroom and fell asleep or something."

"I'm not sure he'll buy that," she gives me a glance, "given this state you're in."

Grace's phone starts ringing again and my heart beats faster. Impulsively, I click the decline button on the screen.

"I thought we weren't declining his calls?" Grace throws up a hand.

"Sorry, I panicked."

I wanted his name off the screen. I feel sick.

A text message dings in on Grace's phone.

"What does it say?" she hands it to me, and I read it aloud.

"Grace. Please pick up. This is not about Emma sneaking out."

The sinking feeling in my stomach shifts from dread to concern. What else could it possibly be about?

The phone rings again and Grace immediately picks it up.

"Hi, Mr. Rivers," her tone is charged with a range of emotions.

"Grace, is Emma with you?" he doesn't give her time to reply before continuing, "I'm sure she is. You both need to get to the hospital as soon as possible."

"Uh, um, yeah, she's with me," she stutters, trying to get the words out as quickly as she can. "What's wrong?"

"It's Eleanor. She was hit by a drunk driver. I don't know any more than that. I don't know how bad it is, but I'm headed to the hospital now."

The concern swirling in my stomach turns to a nauseating distress. The urge to puke I suppressed early comes barreling back up. I motion for Grace to pull the car over. We're on a back road in the middle of nowhere. She quickly pulls to the side of the road and before we're completely stopped, I open the door and throw up on the grass.

"Grace, are you still there?" Dad's voice is filled with desperation.

"Yes, sorry."

I stop throwing up. "I'm here too, Dad. I'm so sorry."

"It's okay. We can talk about that later. She's at Baylor Scott in Uptown Dallas. I should be there in about forty minutes."

"Okay. We will see you there." Grace replies before hanging up the call.

My head feels both entirely empty and filled to the brim with incomprehensible thoughts.

Dad said he didn't know how bad it was. It *can't* be that bad. It *can't* be. I *should* have been there. I *should* have gone to the concert with her. This never should have happened.

Would've, should've, could've… over and over again the angel and devil appear in my mind.

(Devil) *But you finally lived… you took care of you and enjoyed what you wanted for once!*

(Angel) *Your mom was just trying to be nice. She knows you didn't mean what you said.*

(Devil) *Who cares! She'll be fine and you showed her you're not entirely under her rule.*

(Angel) *She loves you. Be there for her now. It's going to be okay.*

(Devil) *Who cares if it's not okay? You do you, boo!*

"Shut up, Devil!" I shout aloud, breaking the silence that has been the last thirty minutes.

I startle Grace and she looks concerningly at me. "Are you okay?"

"Not really." I don't have the energy to expand further.

We make it to the hospital and see Dad pulling in at the same time. We walk in together and I'm thankful he can do all the talking. We're directed to the second floor and asked to wait in the upstairs lobby.

Grace and I take a seat, while Dad paces in front of us.

I want to apologize. I want to tell my dad I am sorry for all of it, and that I'll never act this way again, but it doesn't seem like the right time. He's a patient man. I know he will forgive me. And more than that, I know my mom is his best friend. The only thing in the entire world he cares about right now is making sure she's okay.

A plain looking nurse in blue scrubs comes out of the double doors.

"Family of Eleanor Rivers," she calls, although, I am not sure why because we are the only ones in the lobby.

"That's us," Dad half raises his hand and walks toward her.

"You can come see her now. She's stable."

Stable? That sounds good. Or, at the very least, it sounds hopeful.

We follow the nurse through the winding halls until she stops at a door and lets us in.

Mom's eyes are closed and, if it weren't for the cuts and bruises already forming on her face, she might even look peaceful. The hospital sheet is pulled up halfway on her chest, with her right arm under it and left resting on top in a black sling. Her left eye is swollen with a gash across her eyebrow and the right side of her face looks like a bad carpet burn.

"What happened?" Dad asks the nurse as he walks to stand next to the bed. He softly brushes his hand against her dark, blonde hair.

"A bystander said he saw her walking across the street downtown and a car hit her. The man driving got out of the car, took one look at her, and then left. She was using the crosswalk, and it sounds like the man didn't stop at the red light. Thankfully, the bystander called 911 and got the license plate as well. That's all I can tell you about that though, I am sure an officer will be by soon. As far as her health, she broke her collarbone but doesn't seem to have broken anything else. She's said a few comprehendible words but hasn't been fully awake. Her breathing is stable and we're keeping a close eye on her vitals."

Too much to process. Too much beating around the bush.

"Is she going to be… okay?" I want the facts.

"We're going to keep a close eye on her," the nurse evades the question. "You're more than welcome to stay here with her, though I do recommend getting some rest. It could be a long road ahead and it's late. Being tired on top of all of this won't help anything."

And neither will being drunk.

As if I could possibly sleep right now.

"Thank you," Dad says, and he sounds genuine.

"Please let me know if you need anything. You can press that button to call me. I'll be back in a little bit to check on her." She points to a red button next to Mom's bed and leaves the room.

"Eleanor," Dad holds Mom's hand and kneels by the bed, "I love you."

I see Mom's arm move ever so slightly. She squeezes his hand.

* * *

The hospital room is bright with light streaming in from the windows when I wake. I find myself on the small couch in the room with a thin blanket on top of me. I don't remember falling asleep.

Dad is sitting in a chair next to the bed, still holding Mom's hand, his eyes drooping. I'm guessing he didn't sleep at all.

Mom has a mask over her mouth with a tube coming out of it that wasn't there last night.

"What's that?"

"They put her on a ventilator about two hours ago.

Her breathing was a bit shaky, and they wanted to stabilize it."

I guess I was sleeping pretty hard if I didn't hear any of that.

"Oh, has she been awake at all?"

"No. She's squeezed my hand a few times when I've talked to her, but she hasn't opened her eyes."

Suddenly, I feel my stomach turn and I throw my hands to my mouth.

Dad sees my face go pale. "The bathroom's right there." He points behind him.

My head starts pounding as I quickly move to the door. After losing what feels like everything in my stomach, I return to the room. I take a seat on the couch again and rub the bridge of my nose with my thumb and finger. So… this is what a hangover feels like.

"Do you want to take my seat?" Dad offers, "I was thinking about going to the cafeteria to get us some breakfast."

"Yeah, I can do that." I'm thankful he still isn't forcing a conversation about my poor choices, given my current state.

"What do you want?"

"Whatever is fine," I shrug. I know I should eat, and I can feel my stomach on the edge of a growl, but I don't feel hungry.

"Okay, I'll be back in a few." Dad stands up and leaves the room.

I make my way to his seat. It's warm, and I don't like the feeling, but it passes quickly.

I grab Mom's hand and it feels limp in mine.

I'm surprised by the immediate lump that forms in my throat. I guess the sobriety is finally letting me feel my emotions. Tears begin flowing from my eyes. My mind races with a million thoughts, and I want to say something, but I can't form any of the thoughts into words.

I don't know how long Dad is gone, but when he gets back, he eats first, and I continue to hold Mom's hand. Nothing else matters. After a couple of hours of repeated excuses and delays, Dad finally forces me to eat something and take a break from her side. I switch seats with him and open the Styrofoam container to find cold, soggy French toast covered with syrup and a room temperature yogurt.

"They're probably serving lunch by now, if you want to get something fresher," Dad offers, seeing my nose turn up at the container.

"Probably a good idea."

He hands me his wallet and I go to the cafeteria. It's relatively busy and everything feels like a blur around me. I mindlessly pick out a tuna sandwich and chips before heading back to the room. It occurs to me only upon sitting back down that I don't particularly like tuna fish, but I don't really care. I'm too stressed to think about anything at all.

"How are you doing today?" Dad asks, still seated next to Mom's side.

Mom replies with a thumbs up. I feel a sense of hope: she's responsive. She can hear us. Then, jealousy rears its ugly head: she never even squeezed my hand and Dad gets a thumbs up? She hates me. She remembers last night, and she *hates* me.

* * *

"Hey, how is she?" I hear the panicked voice of my brother start talking the moment he enters the hospital room.

My heart sinks. I didn't even know he was coming home from college. This must be worse than I'm letting myself believe.

"She's okay," Dad softly replies. He's been next to Mom all day, except when we've been asked to leave the room for testing. He gets up to let Bennett take his seat. "She gave us a thumbs up about eight hours ago, but that's the last sign of responsiveness we've seen."

Us? Yeah, right. She gave me no signs of responsiveness. She's only responded to *you.*

"Hey, Mom. I'm here. We're all here," Bennett says as he sits down and rubs her arm gently.

What happened to him? It's only now, with his body facing toward me that I can see his full appearance. His hair is artificially blonder, and it's pulled back in a raggedy man bun. In high school, he was the preppiest, most put together guy in his grade. Class president. Captain of the debate team. Honor student. The whole bit. Now, he looks like he's landed with a group of high-school dropouts all failing at "trying to find themselves."

He looks terrible… which, selfishly, brings me a bit of joy. At least, if Mom wakes up, she'll have something else to focus on besides me.

"Mr. Rivers," a man in a white lab coat, who I recognize as one of the doctors who's been in and out of Mom's room, walks in. "Could I speak with you for a moment?"

"Of course."

Bennett and I don't exchange words or glances while he's out of the room.

When Dad comes back, his eyes are red. He looks distraught.

"What did he say?" I ask.

"They're concerned about the length of time which she's been unresponsive. They ran a few tests early today that showed no activity in her brain. They're going to repeat those tests in a couple hours…" he trails off and I don't know if he's going to be able to finish talking, "And if the results are the same, we're going to have to talk about whether or not to keep her on life support."

"Well, of course, we'll keep her on life support," Bennett definitively replies. "Don't we want to keep her here as long as possible?"

"What? That's no way to live. We don't want her to be…" words come to mind to describe her current state, but they all seem insensitive and wrong, "like this forever." I gesture to her on the bed.

This new knowledge makes her look more lifeless than she seemed before.

"Are you serious? You want to –"

"Stop it!" Dad raises his voice and we're both startled. He never yells. "We're not going to fight about this now… or ever for that matter. We don't even need to discuss anything until the test results are back."

* * *

The nurse comes out and informs us that Louise is stable enough to have visitors, and I'm transported back to the present reality. Respectfully, we let Richard go in alone and check on her first. After another hour or so, he comes out and invites us in. Dad and Grace stay in the lobby, they don't know her that well and don't want to overwhelm her.

I am pleasantly surprised when I walk in the room. I had been expecting the very worst, and instead, find Louise sitting up in bed, seemingly fully alert, and eating cherry Jell-O.

"Oh, come on now. You guys came to check on me?" she seems mostly bothered with the tiniest dose of appreciation.

"Of course, we did. We care about you," Austin replies.

"Everyone makes such a fuss about old people. If I were still forty, no one would be here. They wouldn't have ambulanced me to the hospital, and I'd already be released. It was no big deal. A mere fainting episode..."

"I think they said you had a mini stroke," I correct her, "not a 'mere fainting episode.'" I make air quotes.

"Apples to oranges," she shrugs. "Regardless, I'm fine now and I should be released tomorrow. No big deal and you can all go home."

"Can we get you anything first?" Austin offers.

"I'm fine."

"Are you sure?" I ask.

"Tell you what... if you really insist on doing something. Why don't you bring me one of the mini triple mousse cakes from Croissants? Those are delicious."

She's a woman who knows what she wants, and I

love that about her. "You got it. We'll go and grab that and then leave you alone."

"Sounds good to me."

* * *

We drive down the road to Croissants, which is less than a mile away, pick up Louise's requested cake and head back. I am thankful Dad and Grace are happily along for the ride and don't mind the time we've spent on Louise. Even though they don't know her well, they know me well, and they care about anyone who's important to me.

"Why don't you just run it up to her?" Austin suggests as he pulls up to the main entrance of the hospital. "I'm sure she won't want us to stay long anyway."

"Okay," I grab the plastic bag with the to-go container from the floor in front of my seat. "I can do that."

In the short walk to Louise's room, my mind retreats unwelcomely to the place it left off earlier.

* * *

The hours go by in painstakingly slow agony. We wait what feels like days for the results and are presented with the worst-case scenario: Mom has lost all brain function.

Before Bennett and I can start fighting again, Dad explains how he wants things to be.

"Your mother appointed me as her medical representative in her living will, which means, I will ultimately be the one making the decisions. I do value your opinions and your thoughts, but I will not tolerate hard feelings if I choose to go in a direction different than you wish. It's late and we all need some rest. We're going to go home and get some sleep and tomorrow I will talk with each of you individually and listen to your points of view."

"I don't want to leave her," Bennett and I reply in unison. At least we're on the same page about something.

"She's in good hands here and we will all be better if we take some time away and are able to think more clearly." Dad leaves no room for debate and before I know it, we're back at home for the night.

I hardly sleep, dozing in and out restlessly for hours, until finally the sun starts peeking through my bedroom window. I go downstairs and find Dad starting the coffee maker.

"Morning," I quietly greet him. I can't get myself to add a positive adjective before the word.

"Morning," he replies. "How'd you sleep?"

"Hardly at all," I shrug. "Too much on my mind."

"Me too," he agrees, though he looks relatively put together. His hair is combed, his shirt is fresh and the bags under his eyes seem to have disappeared overnight.

"Is Bennett up yet?"

"I haven't seen him."

"Can we talk now then?" I can't wait any longer to share my opinions.

He hesitates and then sighs. "Sure. Let's go outside."

I take a seat in my favorite chair. It's the one with the best view of the backyard and comfiest cushion. If I were nicer, I'd offer it to my dad, but I'm not, and I need all the comfort I can get this morning. So, I take the good seat and he sits next to me.

"Dad, she can't live like that… it's no life for her… or for you… or for us. It will just prolong her suffering and our grief, and I can't stand to watch her lifeless body like that day after day. If they really thought she'd have a chance to come out of it, that would be one thing… but they said she's brain dead and they're confident she won't come back and I…" a lump wells in my throat, "I can't stand the thought of her breathing with nothing happening up there. Mom's always been so intelligent and witty and clever and bright and… and it's not her without her knowledge. It's… it's just not…" I rub my eyes as tears leak out of them.

Dad gets up from his chair and kneels next to me. He puts his hand on my back and rubs softly. "I understand, Emma Bear. I know where you're coming from.

It's hard for me to see her like that too. It just doesn't feel like it's her."

"So, you agree? Are you going to take her off life support?"

"I haven't fully decided yet and I haven't talked to Bennett. I need a bit more time to meditate on it."

"When are you going to decide?"

"I'm not sure. I don't have a deadline… I mean that's the whole point… we can keep her on it as long as we'd like but I think for the health of our family, it's best to decide in the next couple of days. We need to know what kind of new reality we're going to learn to cope with: a very different one with her or one without her."

* * *

Two days go by, and I only go to the hospital once for an hour. It kills me to see Mom so spiritless. I don't like going there. Dad said yesterday he'd decide today… but the day before he said he'd decide tomorrow, so I am not banking on getting any answers.

Dad hasn't brought up the party or the alcohol and at this point, I doubt he ever will. He knows there's nothing he can say to make me feel worse than I already do. The disappointment I feel in myself and all that's come from that night will never go away.

Ever.

And he can't say anything to make that fact more or less true.

Bennett and I have barely spoken. Despite Dad trying to keep our opinions separate, we both know where the other stands and we're on opposite ends of the spectrum.

It's easy for Bennett to say, "keep her on life support." He's not here. He moved away to college, and he's made it clear he's not coming back home anytime soon, so it's not his responsibility. He won't be here every day visiting her, taking care of her, keeping her company… doing all the hard work. Dad and I would. We'd be the ones watching her suffer endlessly.

* * *

"Emma," Louise's voice impedes my thoughts. "Are you okay?"

I realize I'm standing back in her room. I guess I was walking on autopilot.

"Oh," I shake my head, trying to regain my bearings, "sorry, lost in thought. Here's your cake." I walk toward the bed and set the plastic bag on the table next to it.

"What were you thinking about?"

"Oh, nothing," I nonchalantly wave my hand. "I know you didn't want us to bother you, so I won't stay." I turn to leave.

"Emma, you can talk to me. Are you sure you're okay?"

"Yeah," I shrug, half turning back. "It's… it's just the last time I was in a hospital was when my mom died. My mind is spinning… that's all."

"Oh, dear. I'm very sorry. That's a lot to think about."

"It is." I agree. I turn again to leave.

"Are you sure you don't want to talk about it? A listening ear can save a tear," she smiles.

My heart almost breaks on the spot. Mom always used to say that. I grab a chair, move it to the edge of her bed, and take a seat.

"Well, I know I told you before my brother and I are estranged… and most of that has to do with my mother's death. We… we disagreed on how things should be handled at the end."

I want to stop. I don't want to get into all this… but one look at Louise's soft, wondering eyes and I can tell she won't let me stop, even if I try.

"You see… Mom was hit by a drunk driver after a concert in downtown Dallas one night. She was walking to her car a few blocks away and a man didn't stop at the red light. He hit her on the crosswalk and left. She was rushed to the hospital, battered and bruised. She was relatively responsive the first ten hours or so, but then nothing. They pronounced her brain dead not long after and it was up to us to decide whether or not to keep her on life support."

"Oh, Emma," Louise sighs heavily. "That's terrible."

"And that's not the worst of it… Bennett was adamantly against taking her off it and I wanted to. I didn't want to see her suffer and have no quality of life. In the end, it was up to Dad. He was her medical representative and I found out later they'd talked about it when she was alive. He knew what she would have wanted, and she didn't want to live like that. He heard us out, let us share our opinions and such… he listened but he knew all along what he'd have to do. After five days, he had them take her off life support and she died a few hours later. Bennett blamed me for all of it."

"Because you wanted to take her off it, you mean?"

"Well, that and…" I have only relayed this awful, personal part of the story one other time, and that was to Austin a while back, and he didn't hate me after. I guess I can give it another go. "I got in a big fight with my mom before she went out. She'd purchased tickets to a concert for us and I didn't want to go. I wanted to kiss some stupid boy who'd invited me to his party," I roll my eyes. "Turns out, he didn't even want to kiss me… he wanted to kiss my best friend. Anyway, I told my mom her concert was stupid, and we got in a dreadful fight, which ended with me being grounded and me telling her I hated her. She went to the concert without me, and I snuck out and got drunk at the party. I was a complete mess… if I had gone to the concert, she wouldn't have been hit."

"You don't know that," Louise kindly replies.

"It's okay. You don't have to do that. I've replayed the night thousands of times and there's no healing it. I know I should have been there. I should have been there that night and the days following in the hospital. I couldn't even get myself to say goodbye to her before they took her off life support. I held her hand for a while, but I never even told her I was sorry. I never spoke to her again. The last thing I said to her was 'I hate you.'"

I expect to start crying, but I think I'm too sad. I don't have the energy to form tears. I feel empty.

"She knew you loved her, Emma. I'm sure she did."

"That's very kind of you to say but you really don't have to…" I want the conversation to end. "Richard said he's boarding Daisy until you get home, so it's a bit less stressful for you both. Please let me know when they release you, and I'll come walk her when you need. Let me know if you need anything in the meantime. I'll let you be."

I leave the room, and this time, I don't give her the option to object.

* * *

My head feels heavy on the way home, but my chest feels a bit lighter. I feel something different after telling my story to Louise. Relief? Peace? Sympathy? I'm not exactly sure but I almost feel better.

"I'm glad she's going to be okay," Austin takes a seat on the living room couch.

"Me too," Grace and I agree in unison.

"Excuse me, one sec," Dad picks up his phone and heads back out the front door.

Austin and Grace start talking about some reality survival show they both like, that I never watch, and I opt to scroll on my phone, instead of pretending to listen.

A few minutes later, when their argument over how "last season was rigged" is getting a bit heated, Dad walks back inside and I'm thankful for the interruption. Although, the relief doesn't last long.

"Is everything okay?" I ask, feeling a bit concerned about the look on his face.

"Um… yeah," he puts his hand to his mouth and rubs his chin. "I… uh… I have some crazy news."

"What is it?"

Austin and Grace have noticed the shift in the mood and stop their ranting to listen.

"Well… when we got to the hospital, and I heard Louise's last name… I oddly thought it rang a bell. I called Melissa, my assistant," he adds for Austin's benefit, "and had her go to the house and look through some files. As it turns out…" he pauses, his eyes wandering, as if they're searching for an unknown entity.

"What?" I prod.

"Louise… um… I think Louise was the recipient of Mom's heart."

FIFTEEN

This Simply Cannot Be

"What?!" my mind is suddenly spinning. "How can that be? What do you mean?"

"Your mom was an organ donor. Not long after she passed, I received some information regarding her transplants, but I didn't pay much attention to it. Some people find comfort in knowing but, to be honest, it sort of freaked me out. She ended up being a viable candidate for organ donation and she saved five people's lives."

I think he's going to keep talking but it's already too much to process. I interrupt, "How did I not know this? I didn't even know she was an organ donor."

"I told you at the time," Dad shrugs. "There was a lot going on. It wasn't a major focal point for us… and like I said, I wasn't totally sure how I felt about it. I over-heard Richard say something to Austin about her heart history and I really got to thinking. I called Melissa when we were at the hospital to start looking into it and she found her name. I know it sounds wild… but I have an odd feeling it's true."

"You really think that out of the nearly eight billion people in the world, Mrs. Rivers' heart was transplanted to Louise? That's insane," Grace voices all of our doubts.

"There could be tons of Louise Walters in the world," I add to Grace's point.

"On it." Grace starts typing away on her phone. "There's a site that estimates how many people in the world have a given name… Lo-ui-se Wa-lt-ers," she slowly speaks aloud as she types. "It looks like there are 15,273 people with the first name 'Louise' in the United States and 185 people with the last name 'Walters' and seventeen with an exact first and last name match… which means there's a 5.88% chance it could be her."

Grace doesn't strike people as the kind of girl who would be good with numbers, but she's incredible at them. I would never double check her math.

"Do you know anything about this?" I turn to Aus-tin, suddenly remembering he's known Louise essentially his entire life.

"I don't know much about her health history… I know she's had a couple of major surgeries, but I didn't even know, until Richard mentioned it today, that they were heart related."

"Would they even fly an organ out here? Don't you think they'd give it to someone in closer proximity?" Grace brings up a good point.

My brain falters for a split second and my heart comes seeping in with emotions. What if Mom's beating heart is really in Louise? What if a part of her is still alive? What if Louise really is my guardian angel?

"I have no idea," Dad sighs. "I know this is a lot to take in and it's a pretty out there assumption… but what if it really were true?"

"It would be quite serendipitous," Austin winks at me and I smile.

It would be truly serendipitous indeed.

* * *

We spend the next hour looking up information about organ donation and trying to find anything helpful we can about the process. We agree it's best to check into the *possibility* it could be Mom's heart before talking to Louise about it… it seems a bit too vigorous a conversation for someone who's just had a mini stroke.

We do find out it is possible, though not necessarily likely, that a Texas heart could be flown to South Carolina. We also find it's much more difficult than we anticipate learning about the subject… one would think the information would be more readily available for such a life-saving opportunity.

"How old would Louise have been?" Dad asks. "I see on here transplants are rarely performed on anyone over the age of sixty-five."

"Uhh…" I try to do the mental math. She turned seventy-five in January and Mom died in March eight years ago, "soo sixty-seven."

"Hmm… well, it says it's rare to be over sixty-five, but they perform them on patients up to seventy years old, so not impossible. Especially if she didn't have any other health concerns."

"Ugh," I let out a big sigh. "What are we going to do? What are we possibly going to find on the internet that will confirm this for us?" I answer my own question. "Nothing."

"She's right," Grace quickly agrees. "We can go around and around in circles here, but we've spent an hour and we're right where we started. All we know is that it's a real possibility that Louise received Mrs. Rivers' heart."

"What do you want to do? Ask Louise about it?" Dad sincerely suggests.

"Ugh! I don't know what I want to do… but I do know that I don't want to do that yet. What if you ask your grandparents if they know anything?" I suggest to Austin. "I mean, what if they know she had a heart transplant in the last ten years? That would be pretty convincing evidence."

"I can call my grandma right now, if you want?"

"What do you guys think?" I look to Dad and Grace.

They both nod.

"Be right back," Austin grabs his phone and steps out onto the balcony.

Five minutes later, he comes back into the apartment, and we all stare with ardent curiosity; patiently waiting for whatever news he might bring.

"Believe it or not, Grandma confirmed Louise had a heart transplant surgery a number of years ago. She said she helped the Walters take care of things around the house for a while after it."

My heart feels like it could beat out of my chest. Maybe I'm the one who needs the surgery, though that's probably not something to joke about.

This can't be.

What are the chances? There are literally more than seven billion people in the world. I only talk to like four of them. One of them is a seventy-five-year-old woman.

And that woman just so happens to be the one who received my mom's heart?

Impossible.

Incredible.

"Now do you want to talk to Louise?" Grace's tone suddenly implies she knew it was true all along, like I should have been okay talking to Louise an hour ago.

"Should I go to the hospital? What do I say? 'Hey, I think you have my mom's heart?' Like it's the most casual statement… like I might as well be saying, 'Hey, I think we should order pizza tonig –" the thought of pizza reminds me of something I'd read while researching heart transplants: "recipients often take on attributes of their donors, such as changes in tastes and food preferences."

"Emma? You okay?" Dad questions.

"Yeah… it's just that I think she really does have Mom's heart."

"What makes you say that?" Grace asks.

"I read online that recipients can often like the same foods as their donors after the transplant… Mom loved hot honey on her pizza. It was the weirdest thing, but she wouldn't eat pizza without it. She carried a bottle of honey in her purse with her 'just in case' pizza was ordered. I've never heard of anyone else doing that… or better yet, I never *had* until Louise did it. She told me she'd only discovered the combination a few years back and now she's obsessed."

"Wow… that's… crazy." Austin comments.

"This is all crazy," I agree.

Grace abruptly changes the subject. "I just looked it up and the visiting hours of the hospital ended at 8:00 p.m. It's already a quarter past, so you can't go tonight. Maybe you could go first thing tomorrow? They start at 8:00 a.m. That would give us all some time to decompress and think of the best way to broach the subject."

"That's a good idea," Dad affirms.

"Yeah, I think so too," Austin adds. "I guess I just have one more question though… why are you concerned about asking her? Are you worried she'll be upset? Don't you think she'd think it's as mystifying and incredible as you do?"

His questions stirs the sentiment I've been pushing down since Dad first broke the news.

I already lost Mom once. If part of her really is still alive in Louise… I don't know how I can go on.

I simply cannot bear to lose her again.

* * *

Somehow, I manage to get some sleep overnight. The morning is a blur with Dad, Grace, and Austin all presenting their finest thoughts to me. I kindly pretend to listen, but I know I won't take any of their advice… or maybe, technically, I will… if I end up saying what they say I should… but I am planning to wing it. How can something so emotional be so logical? It can't. It's like trying to fit a square peg in a round hole. Impossible… just like this entire situation.

It's times like these I wonder how people cannot believe in God. Or at least any god for that matter? How can people go through life believing there isn't a greater force out there? A force pushing and pulling us closer to one another. Connecting us all in miraculous ways.

I know Louise is not a morning person, so I wait until around 10:00 a.m. to leave for the hospital. I expect the time to creep by, considering I woke up at 5:00, but it doesn't. It ticks on at its usual pace, though time is relative… but I can't go down that rabbit hole right now. Focus, Emma.

I pull into the hospital parking lot and concentrate on my breathing as I walk to the hospital room. What really would change if Louise has Mom's heart? I'm not sure… but I'm about to find out.

"Hi, Louise," I tentatively greet her as I walk in the room. I'm sure she'll be upset about my coming back to the hospital today and making a big deal of her being here.

"Emma? What are you doing here? I told you yesterday I –"

"I know, I know. I'm sorry… I actually came to talk to you about something." I might as well cut to the chase… no use beating around the bush. I pull a chair up next to her bed and take a seat.

She adjusts the pillow behind her and sits up a little straighter. "What's that? Is this about my health? If Richard sent you here to talk to me about getting a full-time nurse at home I swea –"

"Louise, no," I wave my hands and interrupt her. The same bluntness I love about her is about to drive me crazy. I just want her to let me talk. "I actually have some pretty crazy news… or questions or… I don't know. I'm rambling. I guess for starters… I was wondering… did you ever have a heart transplant?"

Louise furrows her brows, taken aback by the question. "Uhm, yeah, I did actually. What makes you ask that?"

"When was it?" I ignore her question.

"Uhm, probably about seven years ago now. Why do you want to know?"

Again, I ignore her, plowing ahead with my own motives. "But when exactly? What was the date?"

"It was March… uhm… March 26, 2015."

The day after Mom died.

A lump wells in my throat.

This simply cannot be… but at the same time, it must be true.

"I have something unbelievable to tell you."

Louise doesn't say anything but looks back at me, her eyes hazy with intrigue.

"I think your heart... I believe the heart you received was my mother's."

Louise's shoulders relax and she slumps softly back into her pillow. She bites her lip and her eyes squint slightly. She takes the thought in, and I don't rush her. It's a lot to process.

"Well, isn't that something," she finally breaks the silence.

Isn't that something? I don't know what I expected her to say but it wasn't that. Of course, it's "something." Everything is "something." Even nothing at all is still "something" because it's "nothing."

"I... I'm sorry if that makes you uncomfortable or upset. I... I shouldn't have said anything." I reach to grab my purse and start to stand but Louise's hand stops me.

"Emma, what on earth are you doing?"

"This is too much for you. I understand... I'm just the girl who walks your dog and I've inserted myself much too firmly in your life... I've overstepped and I'm sorry." All my fears come spilling out. I hate getting attached to people and now here I am, anchored to Louise's sail. The ocean much too deep... but if I swim away now, I might not drown.

"Emma, please sit down, dear," her voice is firm and calm. It leaves no room for disobedience. I abide. "Emma, you have to see things from my point of view. Take a minute. Let me walk you through this…" she pauses. "A young woman, whom I care about very deeply, just came into my room and gave me a reason to care even more deeply about her. This girl, who I've felt incredibly connected to from the moment I saw her, confirmed that connection. She just told me a piece of her mother lives on in me. Really, it's more than that, a piece of that girl lives on in me. It's an unbelievable state-ment. An unbelievable thought that God would connect us this way. Yet, nothing in my life has ever made more sense."

My eyes fill with tears. I stand up and wrap my arms around Louise. I cry into her. I can't discern the reasons for my tears. There's probably a million of them.

* * *

"How did it go?"

"What did she say?"

"How was it?"

The living room is filled with questions before I even have a chance to shut the door behind me. My face feels flushed, and my eyes feel heavy. I'm both emotionally drained and filled.

I hang up my purse before taking a seat on the couch. I can feel their eyes quietly staring me down, waiting for a summary of the conversation.

It feels easiest to start with the most pressing information, there's no reason to wait to share.

"It's true… Louise was the recipient of Mom's heart."

"Really?" Austin is the first to speak. "How do you know for sure?"

"Well, for starters, she received her heart transplant the day after Mom died, March 26, 2015. But, in an effort to not get too emotionally in the trenches and find out the coincidence alone was wrong, she called Richard while I was there. It turns out, she had received an envelope from the donor alliance that connected them not long after the surgery. She never opened it. I asked her why and she said she'd enjoyed imagining the person whose heart she received. For a while before the heart became available, she'd been getting weekly blood transfusions and each week, she'd tell Richard the kind of person whose blood she received. Some weeks she'd swear it was an NFL quarterback, she felt strong and unstoppable. Others, she'd swear it was some dinky kid whose glasses were too heavy on his nose. She took the same mentality to the heart transplant. She didn't want to know because it made it too real. If she knew nothing, not even a name, she could imagine whoever she wanted to be. She didn't have to think about the person the world had to lose in order to save her."

Dad smiles, "That sounds like something your mother would have done."

"I know," I can't suppress the giddy grin radiating on my face. "I asked her what she'd imagined of her heart donor over the years, and she said she'd imagined her donor to be a relaxed hippie. She pictured her with a go-with-the-flow attitude and a 'life is good' sticker on the back of her Volkswagen bus."

"And what did you say to that?" Dad asks, one eyebrow raised.

"I busted out laughing and I told her she wasn't very good at her own game."

"I loved your mom… but she was none of those things," Dad chuckles. "She was not 'relaxed'… don't get me wrong, she loved to have fun, knew how to laugh at herself and loved to dance… but 'go-with-the-flow' she was not. And I am not sure if she could have imagined a worse vacation than a taking a hippie bus on a road trip through the United States."

Grace joins in our laughter and I can tell Austin doesn't quite know what to think.

"I wish you could have met her," I lovingly reach for his hand. "She would have loved you."

"She really would have," Grace adds and Dad nods in agreement.

"I would have loved to meet her."

SIXTEEN

Everything and Nothing

People always say 'time flies' and quite honestly, I used to think they were kidding.

When I was a child, years ticked by at an unbelievably slow pace. School days never seemed to end, and summer always felt an eternity away. Then, after Mom died, it moved even slower. The days were agonizingly long as emotions flooded me. It felt impossible to keep afloat each day. I couldn't bear to think about swimming for an entire year.

Yet now, here I am, a week before my wedding day, and I wonder how it's all gone by. I've lived each day. I've been with myself the whole time… yet, how did I get here? How has it all happened so fast?

I could swear it was yesterday I started high school

and in the same breath, I barely remember my time there. And wasn't it just last week I met Louise… and Austin? What about Mom dying? Wasn't she braiding my hair and singing me nursery rhymes last month? Relative. Time is relative, and quite frankly, it's relatively a thief. Where has it all gone?

I'm not exactly sure how I expected things to change when I found out Mom's heart was in Louise. I guess there was a small part of me that hoped it would be a fairytale ending. I hoped it would make everything easy and effortless, like it was the only closure I'd ever need. Like it would heal all my years of grief.

But the unfortunate reality is that it's made it harder in many ways. I can no longer see *just* Louise. Every time I look at her, I see a broken part of me. A part of me that has never healed. She used to be a place of refuge. A place of simplicity and an emblem of easy friendship.

But now, it's more complicated. My life feels intertwined. I feel both an agonizing jealousy and an unfathomable sense of gratitude that Mom's heart beats on in her. It's complicated. Life is complicated.

"Are you ready?" Grace's question interrupts my spiraling thoughts and I'm thankful for it.

"Yep."

"Perfect. I don't remember if I told you or not, but I told Louise we'd pick her up on the way." She grabs her keys and purse.

"I'm sorry... you what?" I follow Grace out the door, trying to make eye contact with her.

She evades my eyes. "I invited her. I thought it would be nice if she came along."

"Grace! Why would you do that? This is supposed to be a special day. It's complicated with her now... there are too many emotions and I don't want to process them all." I stand next to her car, arms crossed, refusing to get in.

"You're being ridiculous, Emma. Nothing has changed. She would love to be there."

"Nothing has changed?! Are you out of your mind?" I raise my voice. "*You* moved here, and *you* put my name on a flyer to walk strangers' dogs and *you* started all of this and now you have the audacity to say nothing has changed? Everything has changed!"

"Emma," Grace looks around, noticing we've caught the attention of a few of our fellow residents. "Can we at least finish this conversation in the car?" she asks quietly.

"Fine." I begrudgingly get in. "But don't start driving. I'm still not sure if I'm going."

"I know I started all of–"

Even if that's the start to an apology, I don't care. I still have a lot to say.

I interrupt, "Grace, my life was simple here without

you. It was boring in the best way. I didn't depend on anyone, and no one depended on me. But you… you… you came here and blew it all up. I don't know what to think of it anymore. It's messy and complicated and–"

"And also, kind of wonderful," it's Grace's turn to interrupt. "You can't deny the fact that everything has changed for the better. You met Austin, the love of your life, whom you get to marry next week, and you met Louise, who somehow, out of everyone in the world, is the one person who received your mother's heart. AND you get to hang out with your best friend all the time…" She obnoxiously adds at the end. "How is that not change for the better?"

"Grace…" I sigh. "Okay… I *will* admit in many ways my life has changed for the better."

"Then what's the matter, Em? What has you tied in a knot? Why don't you want Louise to come today? I thought you loved Louise. What changed?"

"That's the *exact* problem, Grace. I *do* love Louise. I care for her so deeply and I hate it. I hate it because I'm completely and irrevocably attached to her…" I take a deep breath, deciding if I'm ready to finally voice the thought that's been eating at me since we found out. "I can't lose her, Grace. I can't lose her… and lose my mom all over again. That's a grief too terrible to fathom."

"But why is *that* what you're focused on?" she doesn't skip a beat and I realize she already knew my fear. She was just waiting for me to admit it. "Why are you focused on the possibility of future grief when you could instead be focused on the time you have with her now?" she shakes her head in disbelief. "You don't always have to be so negative, Emma. I know it hurts, the thought of losing her, but why feel that hurt now? You make your pain worse. You sit in the agony. But she's here. Louise is here and she loves you and she wants nothing more than to make you happy and see you happy. Your mom is in her... literally and figuratively... relish that for everything it's worth because someday, it will be gone. She will be gone... but don't push her away now... not while you still have the blessing of time with her."

Wow. Grace really dropped the mic on that one. How did I not see it that way before?

"You're right," I whisper like a child who is finally ready to admit defeat. "You're right."

"Damn right, I'm right," Grace puts the car in reverse and speeds out of the parking lot. "That's what I'm here for." We ride in silence to get Louise and when she gets in the car, my heart aches. Why have I been pushing her away? She looks fragile. She looks broken. She looks beautiful.

I need more time with her. I need every minute to count.

* * *

"You can come with me," the young, brown-haired girl with an abundance of enthusiasm places her hand on my back, "And you two can take a seat here," she gestures toward a purple, velvet bench.

She leads me through a hallway lined with mirrors and doors to fitting rooms, until we reach one at the back with a chalk sign reading "Emma," hanging beside the curtain. She opens it up to reveal my wedding dress hanging on the back wall. It's even more beautiful than I imagined it would be.

She helps me change into the white dress. It's covered with lace and speckled with immaculately beaded details. The off-shoulder neckline is a sheer-lace with a nude backing and its A-line silhouette flares out gradually from the waist until it reaches the ground. Its appearance is deceiving, because despite the details, it feels lightweight and flowy on me. The back drags slightly behind me and I have to carry the front, in an effort to not step on it, as I walk.

She leads me through the hall again until I am back in the main fitting room. I step up onto a small, circular pedestal and only then do I get up the nerve to look at Grace and Louise's reactions. They're both tearful.

"Wow," Grace comments. "They did an amazing job."

"You look absolutely stunning," Louise agrees.

I take in my reflection in the abundance of mirrors. Even I can't find a flaw in my appearance in this moment… and that's really saying something. I guess a bride's glow really is something unlike any other.

"I love the back. The detail… and those buttons… it's spectacular." Louise compliments.

"Did you bring your veil? Do you want to see it all together?" the bridal consultant asks.

"Yes," Grace answers for me. She gets up from the bench and brings over the veil.

My hair is in a very messy bun. I didn't think about doing it for the appointment, though I guess I should have… other people are probably much better at being a bride than I am. The girl tugs a little at my hair before pressing the hair comb hard into my head.

I chose a simple, tulle veil that reaches down to my midback. I didn't want to take away from the beauty of the dress.

"Have you seen the before pictures?" I ask Louise, fully knowing I never showed her.

"I haven't," she shakes her head.

"Will you show her?" I look to Grace. "My phone is in the top of my purse." I point to the floor by their feet.

Grace unlocks my phone and scrolls through the photos. We've looked at the picture a thousand times while planning the wedding, so it doesn't take her long to find. She hands the phone to Louise.

"Oh my goodness," any tears she'd managed to hold in come flowing out. "You didn't tell me it was your mother's dress."

"You still recognize it?"

"Of course. You can see it in all the details. I see they changed the neckline slightly… probably a good call to get rid of that dreadful 90's trend… and I can see they switched out some of the materials on the bottom of the dress to make it a bit lighter, more modern…" She looks up and down from the phone to me and back as she talks. "And probably a good call to pick your own veil. I'm not sure how that headband style would look with your haircut… Wow. This is really special."

"I know. The seamstress did an amazing job."

"Not just the dress. Everything. I can't believe I get to be here with you," Louise stands up and focuses on gaining her balance before slowly starting to walk toward me. "You look absolutely stunning. I know I can never replace your mother but thank you for letting me try.

What a wonderful moment to be a part of. What a special day it will be."

She stands next to me, making eye contact through the mirror, and I see my mother in it all. In myself. In the dress. In the room. And of course, in Louise.

SEVENTEEN

Highs and Lows

Of all the things I've done in my life, this one might be the craziest. The last six months have been unbearable and breathtaking, miserable and mesmerizing. The highs and lows, the ebbs and flows… they've been too much to handle, and this morning was my breaking point.

Or maybe, it was the opposite? What's the opposite of a breaking point? A mountain top moment? I don't know. I'll have to look that up later.

Right now, I just need to run.

I woke up early this morning and told Austin I needed to go to the grocery store for an emergency woman issue… I knew he wouldn't ask questions. I went to the store and thought about returning home. I thought about telling Austin everything on my mind and asking for his help fixing it… but I didn't. I drove to the airport instead.

And now, I find myself on a flight. I don't know where I'm going… at least that's what I keep telling myself… but I know exactly where I'm headed.

I get off the plane and keep my phone on airplane mode. I don't want anyone to contact me. I don't want anyone to know where I am. This is something I have to do alone. I have to find a way to be okay.

After nine years and twenty-five days, I've finally come to terms with what needs to happen.

I rent a car and start driving to the place I dread most. I almost turn around three times, but I don't, and now, I find myself staring at the ground, struggling to look up. When I finally get the courage, I lift my eyes and read the headstone:

ELEANOR MAY RIVERS

JANUARY 16, 1970 – MARCH 25, 2015

BELOVED WIFE, MOTHER, DAUGHTER & FRIEND

ROMANS 8:38-39

I take a deep breath before I start talking.

"Hey Mom, it's me… you'll never believe the last year I've had… or really the last nine. I'm sorry I haven't been here before now. I know you're not here," I awkwardly gesture at the ground, "you're long gone, and I know I played a part in that and I'm so sorry. I'm sorry I never said I was sorry. I'm sorry I didn't spend more time with you. I'm sorry I didn't appreciate you enough while you were here. I'm sorry for my attitude. I'm sorry I didn't go to the concert with you and that I said Ellie Nova was lame. She's not. In fact, now more than ever I love her music. It reminds me of you. Everything reminds me of you. I can't do anything without thinking of you…" a lump wells in my throat and I pause to swallow it back down.

"I'm not sorry that I told Dad it was best to let you go. That's the one thing I'm not sorry about. It was unbearable to watch you in pain. Gosh… so much has happened since you left. It would take me forever to fill you in on everything. I graduated from the University of Texas with honors… you would have been proud. After graduation, I moved out to Myrtle Beach. I thought it would be good for me to get a fresh start. Two years later, Grace moved in with me…" I laugh a little. "I know you're not surprised. We're still inseparable. But you know how she is… a little controlling… it didn't take her long to insert herself into my life. We went to get coffee one day and I found my number pasted on a flyer to walk dogs." I roll my eyes. "She insisted I get out and meet someone. She wanted me to get a second job to try to meet a guy… and the worst part is, her plan *actually* worked. It was a bit backwards… but it did. I met a woman named Louise with a corgi. She was really in need of some help, and I felt obligated to give it. She's a lot like you.

"Long story short, everyone in my life apparently thought I needed a man… so Louise coordinated a run-in with her neighbor's grandson… sounds like something you would have done… and, as it turns out, he's the best man I've ever known. We got married in October. I'm Mrs. Austin Mackie now," I let out something that resembles both a chuckle and a sigh. "It's still hard to believe. He's kind. He takes good care of me. He's a lot like Dad… you would love him."

I take a seat on the ground and wrap my arms around my knees.

"And speaking of Dad, he's finally moving to Myrtle Beach. He sold the company two months ago and is retiring… though you and I both know he'll never stop working. He's been good. He misses you… and he struggles a lot with Bennett's disowning us because of letting you go… maybe, you didn't know about that… I'm guessing Dad told you… anyway, he's a strong man. I hope someday he'll open himself up to love again but for now, he's happy and I'm not pushing him."

I take another deep breath and run my fingers through my hair. The wind feels cool against my flushed cheeks. A cardinal flies and lands on top of her headstone and I smile. She always loved birds.

"I have the most unbelievable news for you… honestly, you can't even fathom it. When I started walking Louise's dog, I felt a connection with her. She was warm and inviting, yet she seemed lonely. I felt like I needed to be there for her… I *wanted* to be there for her. She told me I was her godsend… her guardian angel but the whole time she felt like mine… and then… here's where it gets unbelievable… as it turns out… she was the recipient of *your* heart." I put my hands to my temples and throw them off, indicating my mind is blown. "Do you know how many people there are in the world? Almost eight billion. And I randomly meet the one who received your heart. I didn't even know you were an organ donor.

"It's been special knowing a part of you is still around… or was… grammar is hard. Getting to hear your heartbeat and feel the warm embrace of a woman who literally carried you with her… it was incredible. She was at our wedding… and my dress fitting… she was where you should have been, and I'll forever cherish that.

"I'll be honest… it was tough at first. I tried to push her away. The reminder was too strong. I didn't want to get attached only to lose you all over again… but the truth is to love is to lose and I wouldn't change a thing."

Tears begin to flow in steady streams down my cheeks.

"She died last month… pneumonia hospitalized her, and she tried to fight for a while, but she couldn't win. She always said, 'getting old isn't for the faint of heart' and she was *not* the faint of heart. She was as tough as they come. In the end, she went peacefully, and I didn't mess it up this time. I didn't make the same mistakes I did with you. I told her I loved her, and I hugged her, and I thanked her for everything I could think of… it still wasn't enough… but I tried. It's been really, really hard, Mom. I can't lie. It's hard to keep going. It's hard to wake up and live each day. Sometimes, I want to throw in the towel and give up, but I don't. I keep going. For you.

"I wish I could go back and change so many things. What I would give to go back to the night of the concert, so that I could go with you. I would protect you from that drunk driver. I would protect you with everything I have.

"I know I can't live my life in the past. And I'm blessed because in many ways, I did get a second chance with Louise, but I know there are things I need to let go. You'd want me to. When we had to decide whether or not to let you go, it was honestly easy. I didn't want you to suffer. I didn't want you to be held down by tubes and monitors and live the rest of your life in a bed. That hardly would have been a life at all… yet for the next nine years, I lived that same way, tied down by my past, unable to let go.

"I needed to come here today to let go, not of you, but of the past that has held me back for so many years. I want to move forward… I *need* to move forward."

I reach into my purse and pull out a white stick.

"This morning, I found out I'm pregnant." I hold the test up. "I couldn't be happier about it. I haven't told Austin yet… poor guy. He's probably worried sick about me. I flew here without telling him. When I saw the two lines this morning, I suddenly realized there's no way I could become a mother without making things right with my own. I wish you could be there when this sweet baby is born." I gently place my hand on my stomach. "I wish you could be here for so many things. I wish you were here for *everything*."

I sit for a few minutes in the silence. Thinking about my mom. Thinking about becoming one myself. Thinking about Louise. Thinking about the pain real, unadulterated love brings.

"I guess what I really want to say I've already said… but you know how I like to talk in circles, and I really want to make sure you hear me. So, I'll say it again… I'm sorry, Mom. I'm sorry for the way things ended between us. I'm sorry for thinking for all these years you didn't love me, and that you died mad at me. I know you didn't. I know you loved me, and I love you. I love you and I promise… I promise this won't be the last time I talk to you. Especially now, I'm sure I'll have a lot to ask you about motherhood… I know I don't need to be here physically to talk to you," I pat the ground. "I can talk to you in the wind, in the waves, in warm chocolate chip cookies… I know you're always around. I know you're looking down on me. I know you're proud of me… and I know it's taken me a long time to know that… but I do now."

I stand up and grab my purse. My shoulders feel lighter. I feel like I can breathe my own breath again.

"I love you, Mom. Talk soon."

EIGHTEEN

So It Goes

The sunroom is sparkling with Christmas lights against the dark night sky. I'm sitting on the couch, admiring the tree glimmering in the corner. I try to soak in the moment of peace in the chaos that has been the last few days. The house is quiet, my hot chocolate is warm, and it's my favorite time of year.

"Hey," Austin peeks his head in. "When is your dad supposed to be here?"

"Uhm what time is it?" I whisper.

He looks over to the kitchen at the clock on the oven.

"5:27 p.m."

"Probably soon. I told him he could come over any time after 5:30 p.m. but I haven't had my phone on me." I shift slightly and think about getting up.

"No, no, I can get it for you," Austin waves his hands for me to stay seated. "Where is it?"

"I think on my nightstand."

He brings it back and a message notification pops in.

(Dad) *I'm heading over now. Worried about traffic on my long commute… LOL*

"He thinks he's hilarious now that he lives down the road." I shake my head and show Austin the text.

He laughs quietly and then softly sits down next to me on the couch. "Can you believe it?" he looks at me with adoration. "The most perfect gift."

"Incredible," I agree.

We sit silently for a few moments until we hear a knock at the front door.

"That must be him," Austin stands up and lends me a hand. The door swings open and lets in a cool breeze of the winter air.

My heart swells with a multitude of emotions as I see my dad, tears already forming in his eyes.

"Hey, Dad." I greet him. "Would you like to meet your granddaughter?" I move my arms slightly to reveal the baby snuggled under a plaid, Christmas blanket.

"Oh my," he softly places his hand on her head.

"She's beautiful."

I carefully shift her in my arms and pass her gently to Dad. "This is Eleanor Louise Mackie."

ACKNOWLEDGEMENTS

My, oh my, it takes a lot to put a book out into the world, and my, oh my, do I have people to thank.

For starters, I want to say a thank you to all the readers who have supported me thus far in my career. It's because of your compliments and encouragement that I want to keep writing and putting out books.

Thank you to my early readers, the ones who read past the spelling and grammatical errors to tell me what they liked and disliked about the story. This final product is because of people like you.

To Taryn, thank you for honest feedback that truly flipped parts of the storyline in my head and gave me a fresh outlook to reorganize pieces of the story (despite losing all your notes and edits).

To Nancy, thank you for everything you've done for me and for the love you've poured into my life. I am forever grateful I nervously agreed to walk Lily all those years ago. Your friendship has meant the world to me. Quite literally, Louise and Emma would never be the same without you (and of course, neither would Daisy).

To Bruce, thank you for moving across the country to be closer to my family and me. You and Debbie have always been inspiring, and you both are interwoven throughout this book more than you could know.

To my grandparents, thank you for taking the time to read the book and make edits, and for unabashedly and proudly promoting my books to everyone around you.

To Jonathan and Molly, thank you for your constant support and encouragement. I am grateful to have you both in my life, and I know I can always count on you for anything.

To my dad, if I could insert two smiling emojis here, I would, and I think that would say enough, but instead, I will simply say thank you for your constant support and grammatical expertise. I don't think I would have a passion for writing, editing, or verbally correcting people's grammar if it weren't for you, and I mean that in the best possible way.

To my mom, thank you for always reading as I write. I can't imagine having to wait days and days (sometimes weeks and weeks) to know what happens next in a story, but you patiently wait for me and encourage me each step of the way. I am forever grateful for our coffee chats and workout plans and laughter over the silliest things in life.

And of course, last but certainly not least, thank you to my husband Josh. You are my biggest encourager, most trusted confidant, and very best friend. I could fill an entire second novel with specific thanks and appreciations to you, but I doubt anyone else would want to read that. So instead, I will simply end with a gracious thank you and a never-ending I love you.

A NOTE FROM THE AUTHOR

When I started writing this book (Easter weekend of 2022), I had no idea all that would follow. I remember vividly sitting on the couch with my husband and pitching him this vague idea that was loosely organized in my head and inspired from various parts of my life. We talked through the general outline and what he liked and didn't like, and faster than I could keep up, my fingers hit the keyboard, and I began writing. Six months later, the first draft was born.

Having worked as both a self-published and traditionally published author, I dreamed of getting an agent for this book. I spent a full nine months querying more than fifty agents and never received a request for a full manuscript. It was a challenging and demotivating season.

I didn't want to put something out on my own again. It seemed too hard and too overwhelming of a task to take on, especially considering the first time around, I didn't have a small child to chase all day. I dreamed of getting picked up by an agent and becoming a *New York Times* bestselling author overnight. I wanted it all handed to me on a silver platter, and I wanted to be able to do it exactly the way I wanted.

I am passionate about writing stories that I believe

in with themes and lessons that reflect my Christian beliefs, while also not being pigeon-holed into "Christian Fiction."

I planned to wait patiently until the right agent came along, but after the sudden passing of a person very, very dear to my heart, I realized I cared more about putting good into the world and sharing my writing (even if it was difficult) than I cared about waiting for the silver platter that might never come my way.

I have put my hypothetical blood, literal sweat, and very real tears into this book, and I am fully aware that all my efforts might never turn into anything bigger, *but* by the same token, if you are reading this, then maybe they have. I want to take the time to sincerely thank you for picking up this book and taking the time to read it. It means more to me than you could ever know.

ABOUT THE AUTHOR

Jesse Maas grew up in the suburbs of Dallas, Texas before moving to Grand Rapids, Michigan for college. After graduating, she lived in Indianapolis, Indiana and Myrtle Beach, South Carolina for many years before finding herself back in West Michigan with her husband and daughter.

Jesse is always up for an adventure (as long as it's scheduled and pre-planned). Her ideas of fun include running, obsessively budgeting (while also spending too much money on coffee), and striving to make the world's best chocolate chip cookies. Not everyone gets her, but she's okay with that. (For enneagram fans, she's a four. Maybe, it makes more sense now).

She is also the author of *Ivy Letters* and *The Desiccant Keepers*.